Jared watched GloryAnn walk toward the clinic.

He'd been so impressed by GloryAnn's competence yesterday, he'd failed to notice how frail she looked. Her oval face now seemed pinched and pale, her big green eyes too large for her face, her jutting cheekbones too pronounced. Would she be up to the clinic's demands?

Then Jared remembered her composure last night when he'd warned her not to get too close to the patients. GloryAnn hadn't liked that, though she had managed to suppress her retort. She might look frail, but he had a hunch she could take whatever was dished out. That was good.

She stood still now, staring out over the water. Jared found himself mesmerized by the perfect peace flooding her face. He hadn't felt that way for a long time—three years, in fact. But maybe it was time to make a change.

Books by Lois Richer

Love Inspired

A Will and a Wedding #8
*Faithfully Yours #15
*A Hopeful Heart #23
*Sweet Charity #32
*A Home, a Heart,
    a Husband* #50
This Child of Mine #59
**Baby on the Way #73
**Daddy on the Way #79
**Wedding on the Way #85
‡Mother's Day Miracle #101
‡His Answered Prayer #115
‡Blessed Baby #152
Tucker's Bride #182
Inner Harbor #207
†Blessings #226
†Heaven's Kiss #237
†A Time To Remember #256
Past Secrets, Present Love #328
‡‡His Winter Rose #385
‡‡Apple Blossom Bride #389
*‡‡Spring Flowers,
    Summer Love* #392
§Healing Tides #432

Love Inspired Suspense

A Time To Protect #13
††Secrets of the Rose #27
††Silent Enemy #29
††Identity: Undercover #31

  *Faith, Hope & Charity
**Brides of the Seasons
‡If Wishes Were Weddings
†Blessings in Disguise
††Finders Inc.
‡‡Serenity Bay
  §Pennies from Heaven

LOIS RICHER

likes variety. From her time in human resources management
to entrepreneurship, life has held plenty of surprises."

"Having given up on fairy tales, I was happily involved in
building a restaurant when a handsome prince walked into
my life and upset all my career plans with a wedding ring.
Motherhood quickly followed. I guess the seeds of my
storytelling took root because of two small boys who kept
demanding 'Then what, Mom?'"

The miracle of God's love for His children, the blessing of
true love, the joy of sharing Him with others—that is a story
that can be told a thousand ways and yet still be brand new.
Lois Richer intends to go right on telling it.

Healing Tides
Lois Richer

Steeple Hill®

Published by Steeple Hill Books™

STEEPLE HILL BOOKS

Steeple
Hill®

ISBN-13: 978-0-373-87468-2
ISBN-10:   0-373-87468-5

HEALING TIDES

www.SteepleHill.com

Printed in U.S.A.

A brother or sister in Christ might need clothes or food. If you say to that person, "God be with you, I hope you stay warm and get plenty to eat," but you do not give what that person needs, your words are worth nothing.

—*James* 2:15–16

For the lovely ladies of Glaslyn whose generous spirits washed over me like a healing tide.

Chapter One

Once he'd written up the charts and the nursing shift had changed, the hospital settled down to its usual midnight calm.

The drag of an overfull day sucked at his energy, but Dr. Jared Steele kept pushing himself to stay awake, kept looking for some sign that their newest patient, a young boy from Venezuela, would make it.

Joy to the world.

The carol poured from the caretaker's radio down the hall.

Christmas—it used to be such a happy time. That last one, Diana had dressed Nicholas up like Santa's elf—

He slammed the door closed on the thought, forced his mind to blank out the pain.

At three o'clock one of the nurses brought a fax from Elizabeth Wisdom.

Sending you help. Best there is. Don't spoil it. E.

He shoved the paper in his pocket, stifled the epithet that rose up his throat. Do-gooders who thought life in

Hawaii would be little more than a beach vacation. Doubtful this one would last three months—like the others.

Jared leaned back in the chair, stretched his legs in front and began rotating his head, trying to ease out the crick in his neck. The boy awoke, watched him.

Jared checked to see if the nurses were around. They weren't. He reached out, picked up the boy's hand. Steady pulse. Good.

"Hey, champ," he whispered. "You're hanging in there. You keep doing your part and I'll do mine, okay?"

The solemn gray eyes blinked.

"Not much of a Christmas for you, is it?"

No response.

"I know how you feel." He rubbed his thumb back and forth over the baby-smooth skin, reminded of another child, one who'd been stolen from him. "Close your eyes and relax. It's okay. I'm here. I'll take care of you."

He kept talking and eventually the boy's lashless lids drooped, his chest moved in a smooth even rhythm. But Jared didn't leave and he didn't go to sleep. And when the boy flatlined he was there to begin resuscitation immediately.

"Don't die on me," he whispered as he pressed the thin chest repeatedly. "Too many have gone already. You have to live."

The heartbeat fluttered back.

"That's right. You can do it. Come on."

But as the dark night grew chilly and shadows moved outside, Jared recognized the signs of his own powerlessness and chafed against it.

"Don't go," he begged. "The world needs kids like

you to make it better." But the boy remained comatose. At four-fifteen the little life began slipping away.

Jared forced the prayer from his heart.

"Don't take him. He's just a kid. His parents have only him." The heart monitor stumbled, came back slower, less responsive. Bitterness welled in a wave so large he could hardly swallow past it.

"You have Nicholas," he said. "Isn't my son enough?"

No answer.

Jared dredged up long-forgotten training, coaxing the frail body to call upon its last resources. By six o'clock he was able to hand over to his assistant, assured that for now, the child would live.

He walked out of the mission to the rocky precipice that overlooked the silver-gilt ocean and watched the flickering rays of sun smear the morning sky crimson. In the caverns of his mind Jared heard a squeaky little voice he hadn't heard in three years.

A voice silenced by a madman.

"Look, Daddy, a boat on Christmas morning. Is it Santa Claus?"

"Why?" he whispered, heart squeezing in misery.

The sun ascended. Humanity awoke. Around the world people were opening their gifts, laughing, loving. But inside Jared's soul lay a barrenness that yearned for answers.

Heaven remained mute.

Two days later

"It's a mission. A hospital for burned children. It's called Agapé and it's in Hawaii."

Dr. GloryAnn Cranbrook struggled to absorb the information. She'd known Elizabeth Wisdom for ten years and never once had she heard anything about a mission. Just how many projects did Elizabeth and her foundation have?

"Hawaii?" she repeated, uncertain she'd heard correctly.

"Oahu." Elizabeth's dreamy smile hinted at fond memories. "I was asked to sit on the board of Agapé many years ago by—a relative."

So Elizabeth was connected to the mission. But Glory knew a lot about The Wisdom Foundation and she knew Elizabeth had no siblings, so this mystery relative was intriguing.

"Agapé has been internationally recognized for its work with injured children." Sixty-plus years hadn't left a mark on Elizabeth's clear skin. "Our mission boasts the latest in equipment, specialized staff, and with Dr. Steele's new grafting procedure, the latest treatment for burned children. Your job would involve working with him as on-staff pediatrician. For six months."

"I did spend a large part of my internship on burn wards," GloryAnn admitted. "I also spent a year studying the psychological effects of physical damage as it impacts a burn victim."

"Because of your mother." Elizabeth's austere face softened.

"Yes. She suffered greatly." Her chest constricted with the ache of loss. "She was the most beautiful woman I've ever known."

Elizabeth touched her shoulder, brown eyes melting with sympathy.

"I know you promised her you'd go back to the Arctic, to the Inuit."

"I have to." GloryAnn knew Elizabeth would understand.

"Of course. But I understand there is now a temporary doctor servicing your village. If you could delay your return by six months, to help the children at Agapé, I'd really appreciate it. Only until I can find a successor."

GloryAnn took a deep breath. There was only one response she could make.

"If that's what you need, Elizabeth, I'm more than happy to go."

"I had no intention of asking you so soon, but—"

GloryAnn leaned forward, covered the long thin fingers with her own.

"You and your foundation gave me back my dream, paid for me to continue at medical school after Dad died, when there was no possible way I could have gone on. I can never repay you for that." She smiled at her benefactor, squeezed her arm. "I'll be happy if I can pass on even a portion of the generosity you've shown me."

"Dear Glory. Thank you so much." Elizabeth enveloped her in a hug perfumed with her favored jasmine. "Of all the women I've selected for scholarships, you've seemed the most like my daughter. I promise you won't regret this decision. In fact, I'm praying that God will use you to do great things at Agapé."

"I don't care about great things. I just want to do His will, to make a difference wherever He sends me," GloryAnn murmured softly.

"And you will, my dear. I know it."

Elizabeth smiled with a confidence GloryAnn envied.

* * *

So this was what paradise looked like in January.

"We are almost there, miss," the driver told her.

"Thank you."

GloryAnn peered out the window, trying to get a better look at her new home. She caught the tiniest glimpse of the Pacific through a labyrinth of volcanic slopes. Honolulu's lights had long since disappeared, leaving polka dots of brightness sprinkled across the surrounding countryside.

The car swung hard to the left. GloryAnn clung to her seat with both hands, hardly daring to breathe as they sped along the winding road. Apparently her driver knew only two ways of driving—fast and faster.

Never in a million years would Glory have guessed she'd be living in Hawaii, even for six months. But how could she refuse Elizabeth's gentle request when the same woman had come to her rescue after her father had died. His death had left her with barely enough funds to pay back the loan he'd borrowed against his life insurance for her first year's tuition money. Elizabeth had been a mentor, a friend and, as it turned out, the only reason Glory had been able to complete her education.

This was Glory's opportunity to pass on Elizabeth's generosity.

A two-story white stucco building perched ahead of them gleamed in the moonlight. It was fronted by a big sign: Agapé. The letters looked as if a child had written them. Underneath, For the Keiki. For the Children.

The sweet, heady fragrance of bougainvillea wafted in, carried by a soft sea breeze that ruffled the American flag fluttering high above the building. Bright driveway lights chased away the shadows. Behind the building Glory saw intermittent red-and-white flashes burst into the sky.

"What's that?" she asked the driver.

"Life Flight. Helicopter. They bring the little ones."

Probably not the best time to arrive. The driver opened the door and held it as Glory got out of the car.

"Thank you," she murmured.

"Mahalo."

She stood for a moment to soak up the sound of swaying palms, pounding surf and whisper-wind.

Aloha, Hawaii.

She followed the driver toward the big glass door.

Inside, the mission was bustling.

"Incoming, Dr. Steele." A woman in a crisp white uniform pulled a cart filled with supplies from a room behind the counter.

"I heard." A tall lean man appeared, short-cropped hair tousled, pale-blue eyes narrowed in concentration. He flung a chart onto the counter, settled his stethoscope around his neck as he moved. He paused in front of Glory.

"Who are you?"

"Dr. GloryAnn Cranbrook. Elizabeth Wisdom sent me."

"About time." He didn't bother with introductions but strode down the hall and out a door without a second glance.

"I'm Leilani Maku." The nurse offered a harried smile. "Welcome to Agapé, Doctor. Do you want me to—"

"Go. I'll follow." Glory grabbed a white coat off a hanger.

The driver had already left. Her luggage was still in

the car but the helicopter's rasping rotors told her there was no time to think about that now.

She hurried after the others, pushing through the door they'd left from. It led to a hallway, which in turn led to a helipad on one side, an emergency ward on the other. She pushed open the outside door and stepped into the night. Dr. Steele was already halfway across the tarmac.

Glory hurried forward.

"What's been done, Leilani?"

His nurse checked her paperwork.

"The fax says they've been typed and matched. I've got a clean room set up for initial assessment. If we need more help, Dr. Sanguri is visiting his mother. He's in the village but he can be here in ten minutes."

"He's an ob-gyn!" Dr. Steele exploded as he waited for the helicopter to land. "He'll be no help."

"He's the only doctor near enough to pitch in immediately."

"I'm here." Glory stepped forward.

Leilani smiled, thanked her. Dr. Steele surveyed her from head to foot, his ice-blue eyes cold as any Arctic wind.

"I hope you can follow directions."

Welcome to Hawaii.

Jared Steele had one hand on the door the moment the helicopter touched down.

"Hey, Doc." A young pilot with a British accent jumped out, helped an accompanying nurse free two stretchers strapped inside. "Meet my friends, Tony and Joseph. Hang on, boys. Nurse Leilani will have you tucked up before you can say Bob's your uncle."

The lilt of his British accent lit up the boys' eyes. Or maybe it was his quick smile.

"What happened?" Dr. Steele surveyed his patients.

"They were at an international kids' event on Maui. Somebody thought it would be fun to douse their campfire with gasoline. The trip here didn't do them any good."

One glance at Dr. Steele's face told Glory he saw what she did—the first child didn't have much time.

"Leilani," he ordered, "get another IV in if you can. Now."

Leilani waved over attendants, who transferred the boy onto the waiting gurney. They hurried inside.

The second boy was wide-awake. Though he looked in pain, he managed to twist his head so he could watch the doctor who was studying his damaged face. Dr. Steele shook his head at the sacrilege, grabbed the edge of the stretcher and began to move.

"Clean room. Stat," he ordered, his voice harsh.

The boy murmured something unintelligible. Dr. Steele glanced at the pilot who was trailing along beside him.

"I can't understand him."

"German. He wants to know if he's going to die."

"We're all going to die."

"That's no answer." The pilot's lips pinched together in an angry line as the two men eased the front wheels of the rolling stretcher through the doors.

"Tell him whatever you like." Dr. Steele glared at the pilot's grip on his sleeve. "Don't they teach you to move when you're asked?"

"Yes, Doctor, they do. They also try to teach us a little human kindness. You should try that."

"Finished?" They glared at each other like leashed pit bulls.

"Yeah, I am."

"Then get out of my way." Dr. Steele pushed the boy forward, his expression implacable.

Glory grabbed the exit door and held it open so the end of the bed wouldn't jar. She followed doctor and patient to the clean room and began treatment automatically, wincing at the extent of the injury. No wonder Dr. Steele was angry.

"I need to see to the first fellow." He rested a hand on the door. "Can you manage here?"

"Yes." She glanced at him, recognized indecision on his face. "I'm fine. Go."

The boy wept silently as Glory worked. The body's ability to tolerate shock only lasted for so long. This one had just about maxed out.

"What did they give him?" she asked the nurse assisting her, mentally juggling protocols.

The nurse read from the chart that had accompanied the boy.

"Okay. Blood pressure's still dropping. Let's go about this in another way." Glory issued new orders, kept one eye on the monitors and worked hard until the child's vitals finally responded.

Working silently, she did what had to be done, but she couldn't stop a tear from trickling down her face, over the mask she wore.

"Don't move him for the next hour. Watch him and monitor everything. If nothing changes he can transfer to intensive care. Understand?" The nurse nodded. Glory stripped off her gloves and gown, stepped out of the room and headed for the first patient. "Anything I can do here?" she asked.

Dr. Steele looked up, frowned. "The other one?"

"Stable. Help or not?" she asked, waiting for his nod before she plunged her hands into the gloves held ready. "Where do you want me?"

He worked frantically, blasting out orders in a terse monotone. She matched her efforts to his. If something didn't happen fast enough he called her on it bluntly.

Glory admired his grit. Lesser doctors might have given up after one code blue, but after three Dr. Steele continued to drive all of them to extraordinary lengths to save the life on the table. Several hours later the boy was finally stable.

For now.

"Okay, he'll do. I want to see the other one now. Come with me," he ordered, barely glancing at her.

"Certainly, Doctor."

Leilani's empathizing smile offered Glory a boost. She returned it then followed Dr. Steele.

"Chart," he snapped at the hovering nurse in the next room.

While she waited, Glory completed another check of his vitals. The boy was doing well.

Hang on, she prayed silently. *Just hang on.*

"Why did you use that particular sedative?" Dr. Steele demanded suddenly.

"I did several rotations at Sick Kids in Toronto. Dr. Lang had a study going that indicated patients had more success with this drug."

"Lang? Corbin Lang?"

She nodded.

"He's good." Dr. Steele closed the chart, handed it to a nurse. He touched the boy's hand just for a moment then backed away. "It'll take time, but right now this one looks like he might make it."

"I hope so." Glory completed one last check before following him to the doorway.

"Probably not the welcome you were expecting."

"That doesn't matter. I'm just glad I could be here to help. I'll bet he was a cute kid before all this happened."

His voice dropped so low she barely heard.

"They all were." A moment later the hint of tenderness was gone. He was all business. "Would you like to look around the wards while you're here?"

"Yes, if we won't disturb anyone."

"Most of them are asleep by now. If we could dispense with the tour tonight it would free up some of my time in the morning."

"That's fine by me. Are either of those new patients candidates for your grafting procedure?"

"No." The clipped answer cut off conversation.

Dr. Jared Steele moved through the wings of the hospital quietly, using only the softest tones to point out the treatments currently in use and the effects of some newer therapies.

"Your success is much higher than standard hospital burn units."

"That's why we're isolated like this. The infections and viral problems rampant in hospitals and so lethal to burned children don't occur here. The climate is perfect for healing and we are able to concentrate on our specialty."

"Yes." She glanced around. "How many doctors on staff?"

"Supposed to be four plus me. Six counting you. They come and go." A sideways glance told her he expected her to do the same. "We're two short at the moment so we take turns rotating shifts. That way everyone gets a break. We don't often get a flight this late but it happens."

"I don't suppose anyone can predict tragedy."

"There are usually three doctors on call but Dr. Xavier left suddenly this morning—family emergency. Dr. Chatter and his wife left without notice a while ago, which is why we're short. Dr. Potter fell ill this afternoon."

"He has dreadful timing."

Dr. Steele did not see the humor.

"You do know the highest burnout rates are among those who treat burn wounds, no pun intended." Those frozen blue eyes constantly assessed.

"Especially when it's children, I know." Glory smiled. "Suffering is difficult to watch, but it's rewarding to see them heal and regain their lives. A hug and some encouraging words go a long way."

"We try for a little more than that at Agapé." His mouth evidenced disapproval. "It's best if you don't allow yourself to get too close to any of the children, Dr. Cranbrook. Most of them are here for a short period of time. Personal attachment only makes the job more difficult."

Glory pressed her lips together. She was a doctor, she knew all about maintaining a professional distance with patients. Dr. Steele made it sound as if she'd fawn over them like some love-starved trainee. Still, he'd had two doctors walk out on him. Maybe he thought the warning was necessary.

"Thank you for the advice," was the best she could manage.

She wanted to ask why the new patients weren't suited to his grafting procedure but there wasn't time as he moved back to the main area, showed her the operating rooms and the treatment areas complete with space-age equipment.

"We have two physiotherapists who come from Honolulu each day. That about sums it up." He sighed. "Your quarters are across the compound. The driver will take your luggage over. Shall I show you where you'll stay?"

Dr. Steele didn't wait for her agreement but told the nurse where he was going then held open the door for Glory to pass through.

"It's not necessary for you to do this. But thank you." She paused outside, let the warmth enfold her. "This is such a beautiful place. I'm sure the children must enjoy it."

"Hmm." His tone didn't welcome further comments.

Glory walked beside him for a few minutes then tried again. "I love the water. Is it safe to swim in the sea here?"

"Quite safe. The cove is protected, meaning the surf won't overwhelm you. The beach and the sea are mostly private, though, of course, we can't forbid anyone to use them."

"You can't?" Intrigued at the loosening of his rigid control, Glory snuck a sideways glance. He was handsome—when he forgot to frown.

"It's an island law one of the Hawaiian kings made years ago and the government upholds it still. No one can own the beach in Hawaii. It is free to anyone who wishes to use it."

The doctor stopped beside a small bungalow.

"This is yours." He led her inside, pointed out a tiny kitchen, bath and bedroom and a glorious garden outside the back door.

"It's lovely. Thank you."

"Mahalo. You are safe here. Agapé's compound is surrounded by a fence and a guard is always on duty—a security measure." He demonstrated how to use the intercom system beside the phone.

"Thank you. I appreciate you taking the time."

Dr. Steele stood under the light of the entry, his blue eyes mixing with hints of silver-gray as they analyzed her.

"You're tired. It's a long flight and the change in climate can take adjustment. Rest tonight. Tomorrow will be soon enough for you to learn the rules of the mission and see to the children's needs. There are a couple of cases I'd like to discuss once you're ready."

"Of course." She inhaled, then pressed on. "I—that is, I was wondering…"

"Yes?" He'd taken a step forward as if he could hardly wait to get away. But he paused courteously, though his face bore an impatient scowl.

"The grafting procedure—I was wondering if you'd be doing it tomorrow."

"No."

The terse response surprised Glory into silence.

He stepped outside, then suddenly stopped and turned back.

"Is there anything else you need, Dr. Cranbrook?" he asked as if he'd been suddenly reminded of his manners. It was painfully obvious he wanted to be gone.

"No, thank you. Good night, Dr. Steele."

"Good evening, Dr. Cranbrook."

Glory detested the stiff, supercilious response surgeons often demonstrated to those they considered lesser mortals, but given Dr. Steele's reputation she supposed he had a right to be conceited.

When he disappeared from sight, Glory stepped back inside her cottage, closed the door and twirled around in the living room, soaking in the thrill of having her own place. After sharing quarters with others for so many years to save money, privacy was something she'd come to crave.

A wave of travel-tiredness swamped her, but Glory-Ann ignored it. In the kitchen she found an insulated decanter and a mug on the counter. A plate with two pale golden cookies and a note sat waiting.

Welcome to Hawaii. May God bless you as you minister to those who need you.
With love, Sister Philomena.

Glory poured out a steaming beverage, smiling at the fragrant aroma filling the air. Mint tea. Her favorite.

"Thank you, Sister Philomena," she murmured. "Whoever you are." She bit into one of the cookies. Lemon. "How could you know what I love?"

She carried it and the tea outside, into a garden filled with scents she'd only ever sniffed inside a florist's. Strategically placed landscape lights lent an aura of peace and tranquillity.

A white wicker chair with a flowered cushion waited beside a small tinkling fountain. Glory sank into it, content to review the day's events. But her thoughts kept returning to Jared Steele, to the craggy harshness of his face as he directed care for the two small boys.

The snap in his response when she'd asked about the grafting troubled her. There was something he hadn't said, something that made her wonder why the other doctors had quit.

But more than that, she wondered why such sadness filled Dr. Steele's eyes.

Glory sipped her tea, peered up at the stars.

Why did You send me here, Lord? she prayed silently. *It's obvious he's got anger issues. He doesn't want to talk about his grafting procedure, but I thought that's why You wanted me to come. So what's Your purpose for me?*

She received no response in the still silence of her heart. But that didn't stop her from pondering why God had led her so far from home, away from her long-held goal to fulfill the deathbed promise she'd made to her mother.

God knew how much she wanted to honor both her parents by returning to the Arctic and caring for the Inuit they loved.

I will go back, Mom, just as soon as I can. I promise you.

Glory had explained her delay to the elders in the village of Tiska. Everyone said they understood. They'd wished her good luck and offered a traditional Inuit blessing.

Now, as the night breeze toyed with her hair, a yearning filled GloryAnn's heart. Leilani seemed nice enough, but Jared Steele was cool and prickly and above all, dictatorial.

It struck her then just how far she'd traveled from everything that was familiar.

Despite the fragrance, the warmth, the soothing lull of the ocean tides, she longed to be back at home soon where ice and snow swathed the land in a thick pure blanket of peace. She ached to hear the howl of sled dogs fall silent and be replaced by the whistle of the Arctic wind as it seeped through the cracks of the house, soothing her to sleep. She yearned to wake to the wide generous smiles of her people, let them fill the empty aching spot in her heart.

She'd been gone too long.

Only six months, okay, Lord? And then I have to go back.

Even Dr. Jared Steele, with his peremptory orders, couldn't sway her from that goal.

Chapter Two

Jared glanced up from his desk through his open window to watch Dr. Cranbrook walk toward the mission.

She occasionally paused, once to pick a small daisy that had pushed its way through the rocky soil, again to smile at a Java sparrow pecking the hardened ground. Then she studied the Kuhio vine Diana had insisted on planting on their anniversary, the first year they'd come here.

He shoved the memory away, mouth tightening as Dr. Cranbrook lifted her face into the wind, allowing her long golden-brown hair to stream behind her. No doubt she, like most tourists, thought this was paradise.

He knew better.

Jared had been so impressed by GloryAnn Cranbrook's competence yesterday he'd failed to notice how frail she was. In the blazing sunlight she now emerged pinched and pale, the big green eyes too large for her oval face, jutting cheekbones too pronounced. Would she be up to Agapé's demands?

Then he recalled her composure last night when he'd

warned her not to get too close to the patients. Dr. Cranbrook hadn't liked his warning, but she had managed to suppress any retort. She might look frail, but he had a hunch she could take whatever was dished out. Good. She might stay a little longer.

She stood statue still, staring out over the water.

GloryAnn—an unusual name but it suited her. Captivated by her look of perfect peace, Jared realized he hadn't felt that way himself for a long time—three years, in fact.

"Hang on to it as long as you can," he wanted to tell her. "What you'll see here will steal your peace away and you'll never feel it again."

But he could hardly say that to Elizabeth's newest protégée. So Jared gathered up his files and waited at the main desk for Dr. Cranbrook to push through the doors.

"Good morning, Dr. Steele. Isn't it a lovely day?" She glanced at the folders in his arms. "Do you prefer to do rounds first?"

"Yes." The building seemed strangely brighter. Jared walked beside her down the corridor, told himself to concentrate on business.

GloryAnn listened as he described each case, glanced at the file for the child's name then struck up some silly conversation with them. It irritated him that she spent so much time talking nonsense when there was so much to be done. The sheath of amber hair falling over one shoulder bugged him. So did the way she met each patient's stare with that reassuring smile.

Finally they arrived at the patient she'd treated last night. She smiled at the boy, held his hand as Jared examined him.

"He's going to need these burns peeled soon." A

giggle from behind him drew Jared's attention to the laughing child. He half turned, caught a glimpse of GloryAnn making funny faces. "Dr. Cranbrook?"

"I heard you." She straightened.

"May I ask what you were doing?"

"Taking his mind off what you were doing." She pulled a small plastic disk from her pocket, showed the boy how to move it so the steel ball inside would follow the path. "You try it, Tony," she encouraged.

Tony did and giggled at his success. GloryAnn turned to Jared, lifted one eyebrow and inquired, "Shall we see Joseph?"

"If you've finished playing."

"For now." She said, tongue in cheek.

Jared fought his impatience down. Her heels clicked on the marble floor. She hummed a little song about sunshine and flowers. Normally, extraneous noise irritated him, but Jared found himself relaxing as the soft melody carried down the hall.

Joseph was in pain. Jared checked him over quickly before increasing his meds. GloryAnn's attention focused on the boy.

"Do you have anything he could listen to?" Her hand grasped the small fingers and cradled them when he moaned.

"I beg your pardon?"

"A radio? A CD player, perhaps? Something to take his mind off his pain when his family isn't here with him?" She paid him little heed, her focus on the boy. "He's going to have to lie still for quite a while. We could make that easier if we gave him something else to think about."

"Such as?"

"Is there someone who could read to him in his language?"

"Dr. Cranbrook, we don't have the staff or the time to entertain—" He stopped midsentence, a rap on the glass window interrupting him. His mother-in-law stood outside, beckoning.

"Not again." She'd already called him twice this morning.

"Dr. Steele?" GloryAnn glanced from him to the woman.

"I'll be a moment. Excuse me." Jared strode to the door, stepped into the hall so Dr. Cranbrook wouldn't overhear.

"Aloha, Jared, *ku'u lei*." *My child*.

At least Kahlia had remembered his request not to enter the room without gowning up. She grasped his shoulders, enveloped him in a hearty hug, something he'd never grown used to from Diana's big Hawaiian family.

"You don't return my calls. How are you?"

"I'm fine. Busy," he added, hoping she got the message.

"You're always busy. Too busy for family." She shook her gray head. "Pono and I are holding a birthday party for Grandma tomorrow evening. You will be there?"

There was no point in arguing with Kahlia, she would only keep nagging him. Diana and Nicholas had been her whole life. She and Pono had doted on their daughter and lavished affection on their tiny grandson. Jared couldn't blame her for needing someone to fill the gap in her heart. He just wished she'd chosen someone else so he didn't have to keep struggling through the reminders of what they'd all lost.

"Grandma's birthday, Jared?" she prodded.

"I'll try."

"Who's that?" Kahlia inclined her head toward the woman now bent over the bed playing some kind of finger game that coaxed a smile from Joseph's parched lips.

"Our new doctor. GloryAnn Cranbrook. She arrived yesterday."

"Lovely. Will you bring her along?"

"I don't think so, Kahlia. She has work to do." Jared took another tack. "Or she could go in my place."

Kahlia's dark eyes scolded. "Always you try to avoid us. We are your family, Jared. We are here for you."

I lost my family.

He clamped his teeth together to stifle the words. Kahlia had mourned enough. They all had. Sooner or later she would accept that he had to get on with his life. Away from here.

"Excuse me, I've been paged." GloryAnn eased past, strode down the hall, hair flying behind her like a silken kite.

"She looks so young, a mere child."

"She's extremely well qualified." Jared barely recalled the list of credentials he'd scanned earlier. "Elizabeth Wisdom sent her to fill in for six months."

"Elizabeth is a good friend to Agapé. Where does this woman go after six months?"

"I have no idea." Jared suddenly realized he knew little about his new coworker. Thankfully he was paged next. "Excuse me, Kahlia. I've got to go. Leave me a note about the party. I'll come if I can."

"But I wanted to—oh, never mind."

Ashamed of his rudeness, Jared bent and brushed her cheek with his lips. "Bye."

By the time he'd dealt with their newest patient and completed two debrading procedures, Jared was more than ready for lunch. He picked up a tray from the cafeteria and moved outside, drawing in deep cleansing breaths and exhaling fully to purify his lungs.

GloryAnn sat on one end of the patio, watching sailboats cruise past their tiny cove. He could hardly ignore her, though at the moment Jared craved nothing more than silence, respite from the weeping children he'd had to hurt to help.

"May I join you?"

"Certainly." She blinked as if awakening from a dream, her smile inviting. "I'm enjoying this weather."

"You'll want to watch your skin. Even though it seems temperate, the sun is strong. A tropical burn is painful, Dr. Cranbrook."

Clearly irritated, she set down her bottle of juice hard enough that a few droplets decorated her fingers. "Why do you always talk to me like that, Dr. Steele?"

"Like what?" Unused to being challenged, Jared froze, his sandwich halfway to his mouth.

"Like I'm a silly child who can't look after herself, let alone anyone else. 'Don't get too close to the patients, watch the sun, don't get the patients too excited with silly games.' It's insulting."

Though neither her voice nor her demeanor changed, anger darkened her green irises.

"I'm sorry if I offended you. I merely wanted to point out that this climate is different than the one you're used to. Sunburn is unpleasant and can be dangerous."

"And you think I don't know that?" GloryAnn put the lid back on her bottle and tightened it so much her fingertips turned white. "I put on sunscreen this morning, SPF 70, and I've been out here—" she checked her watch "—ten minutes. Hardly long enough, don't you agree?"

Jared decided it was better not to answer, so he concentrated on chewing the roast beef he'd selected.

"I assure you I am qualified to be here, Dr. Steele. If you feel that isn't so, or if you would prefer someone else, I suggest you contact Elizabeth Wisdom, because until I hear otherwise I intend to do the job she sent me to do, and I'll keep doing it for the next six months."

She stabbed a piece of lettuce so hard it tore apart.

"Now, since you're here, I'd like to ask you some questions about your procedures this morning."

A new respect filled him. "Fire away."

"I know you like to remove the burned tissue as quickly as possible because that's where infection likes to grow."

"Yes."

"But I've never seen debrading done the way you did this morning. Can you explain it to me?"

Jared explained the process he preferred.

"I'm sure you know that with current procedures it's difficult for surgeons to tell which tissue is dead and needs to be removed and which is still alive and can heal on its own."

"Yes."

"If you've removed more than you need to, that makes it harder for the graft to take. It doesn't heal as well."

"So that machine you were using…?" She lifted an eyebrow.

"It combines laser and radar systems—hence the name lidar. It's something we've been working with for a medical research company—trying to perfect." He babbled on about his work, fascinated by the bloom of color on her cheeks. She was lovely.

"Amazing," she enthused, her smile flashing.

"It is," he admitted. "But it could be even better." He went on to explain the alterations needed. "If they could perfect it, the agony of debrading would become a thing of the past."

"Which would be a blessing for all of us," she muttered, making a face. Her head lifted. "But you can't do that yet."

"No." He swallowed a mouthful of hot black coffee before explaining the need for a laser component.

"What you were doing today with the little girl— active triangulation?"

"Yes." He was surprised by her knowledge. "It's good but prone to errors because light tends to scatter inside the tissue." Jared finished munching on his apple. No point in boring her with his special interest.

"The new machine would be useful for assessing other types of tissue damage?" Those eyes blazed with life, drawing him into them as she spoke.

"Yes."

"Wow!"

Her enthusiasm charmed.

"It has great potential but it isn't perfected yet, so don't start planning any expansions for the mission. Hopefully we'll see some advances soon." He placed the apple core on his plate, noticed the sack at her feet. "Shopping already, Dr. Cranbrook?"

"It's Glory. Or GloryAnn if you must be formal." She glanced at the bag. "I brought a few things from home— for the patients."

"Things?"

"Toys, noisemakers, a couple of handheld games. Stuff like that."

Oh, brother. "Hardly appropriate for Agapé, Doctor."

"Are you kidding me?" GloryAnn surged to her feet, picked up the bag and rattled it. "It's quite appropriate. I've never seen a place more in need of a little joy."

He would have interrupted but she held up her hand.

"I'm sorry. I don't mean to criticize your work, Dr. Steele. I know it is necessary and is helping the kids. But I can't imagine why your last pediatrician didn't suggest doing something to animate the children."

"We haven't had a resident pediatrician on staff for over a year. The last one stayed three weeks. They want everything to be jolly and happy and when it isn't, they don't seem able to withstand the demands this kind of work requires."

Okay, he could have worded that differently, but she'd been here for less than twenty-four hours and she was ready to change all he and Diana had worked so hard to achieve. The knowledge grated like seawater in a wound.

"Maybe you should have hired a different pediatrician," she mused aloud. "I admire your new technology, Doctor. I've seen you work and I know you're diligent and precise. But my purpose in being here is to look after the kids' needs, mental and physical, beyond their burns. I believe they *need* a few old-fashioned toys."

She picked up her tray, paused for a moment. Her face softened, her gaze followed a patient being wheeled along one of the paths.

"I have to start somewhere," she murmured.

Jared's temper flared as he watched her leave the cafeteria. The casual inference that he hadn't done his best for his patients irritated him immensely. He rose, pushed his tray onto the appropriate rack and followed her, quickly catching up.

"Dr. Cranbrook."

"Yes, Dr. Steele." She stopped, lifted one eyebrow in that imperious manner that probably worked well with bratty five-year-olds but simply annoyed him.

"I do not want noisemakers in my hospital."

She stared at him. One corner of her mouth lifted in a half smile, as if she'd caught him out in some prank.

"*Your* hospital?"

Jared swallowed.

"At Agapé, I mean. I guess I think of it as mine because I've been here so long."

"Fresh ideas don't hurt."

Meaning he was a stick-in-the-mud, afraid of innovation?

"No, they don't. But rest is important for these patients. The treatments are grueling, the issue of facing what they look like now can be extremely traumatic."

"Exactly, which is why anything we can do to ease their stress levels, to make them feel normal, is important." She frowned. "Why are you fighting this, Doctor? Surely you must be aware of the connection between positive thinking and the healing powers of the mind."

"Of course. I'm also aware of the benefits of solitude, rest and recuperation and that too much excitement can lead to overexertion and setbacks."

"I'm not talking about too much anything."

Though he felt a fool for calling her tactics into question, Jared refused to back down. He'd gone through this before with eager beavers and it always ended badly. The children always lost. That couldn't happen again.

"I'm chief of staff, Dr. Cranbrook. These children are my responsibility and I don't want anyone trying some crazy idea that's going to interfere with our procedures. The patients need every ounce of strength to get through their treatments."

He turned to leave. Her hand on his arm stopped him.

"Toys? Hardly a crazy idea," she chided, tongue in cheek.

"You know what I meant."

"I do. And I assure you, Dr. Steele, I'm not going to hurt the children or do anything to stop their healing progress. I only want to give them something besides a few dishes of ice cream to look forward to after their therapies are done."

So she'd noticed his attempt to soften the pain. Jared sprouted new appreciation for GloryAnn Cranbrook's shrewdness.

"The pressure suits are agony to put on." Her voice mirrored her sadness. "To face the knowledge that even though you take it off tonight, you'll have to do it again tomorrow—that can prey on the mind and ruin any rest they might get."

"But they're necessary," he blurted out.

"Of course they are. And they make a difference. You and I both know that." Her eyes misted. "But six months, a year ahead—that's a long time for a child to wait to see results. I spoke to some of the nurses. They told me how hard they have to coax some of the older ones to wear the masks."

"Then you also know that the best way to keep their healing skin from drying out too quickly, and to keep out infection, is to wear Lucite masks almost twenty-four hours a day." He was so weary of the reminder that with pain came healing.

Pain hadn't helped him heal.

"They're custom-made for each child to be as comfortable as possible."

"Yes, I know." Her chin lifted, her voice lowered. "You're doing your best to give them a fighting chance, Dr. Steele. I realize that."

"I—"

"All I'm asking is that you let me do the same. I've talked to the physiotherapists. We've come up with some ideas we think will help motivate them. Kids are used to running, screaming, jumping. To be silent and quiet all the time isn't necessarily healthy."

Hard to argue with truth. Jared had seen the brooding set in, watched as the will to keep going faded when the painful treatments never seemed to end.

"There will still be periods of silence," she assured him. "No one's rest will be disrupted, I promise. Maybe they'll rest even better."

Jared had always left this end to Diana. He was a surgeon, used to shutting out emotions, cutting and piecing without really thinking about the patient as a person. In fact, Jared didn't understand kids most of the time. Hadn't really wanted to until Nicholas.

Now whenever he lifted a scalpel, the child on the table became the son he had to save.

"Fine." He agreed so he could get away, stop being reminded. "You can try it your way for a week. But if it doesn't work or if someone becomes disruptive, we go back to the way it was."

"Of course."

A helicopter broke the silence of the afternoon.

"I hate that sound." Jared strode back to the desk to see what new damage had been done in a world where God seemed to have fallen asleep.

Two weeks later, after lunch, Glory climbed up the pathway from the beach feeling both refreshed and at ease.

"I love this ocean."

"Oh, me, too." Leilani poured sand out of her up-turned shoe, grimaced.

"I don't understand how you can live in a place like this and not spend every spare moment beside the sea, if not in it."

"Maybe if I had hair like yours that dried in a beautiful wave, I would, but all I end up with is a frizzy mess that won't stay put no matter what." Leilani unwound the scarf on her head to prove her point.

"Okay then." GloryAnn tilted her head to one side, thinking. "Maybe you should stop having perms."

"And wear what—mop strings? My hair sticks out in all directions. Dr. Steele would send me home."

"Ha! You're irreplaceable. Is he always so—" Glory-Ann remembered who she was talking to and bit off the adverb.

"Cranky?" Leilani giggled at her arched brow. "Well, if the shoe fits." Mirth was edged out by a sad smile. "Ever since his family died."

"He had a family? I mean, I heard he'd been married once, but—" Glory gulped. "What happened to his wife?"

"She died. Was killed, actually." Leilani sat down on a big rock, pulled out her water bottle and took a sip. "Both Diana and Nicholas—their son. He was three years old."

"Oh, how horrible!" A gush of sympathy overtook Glory. She wondered how Jared could bear to stay.

"That's not all." Leilani shoved her sunglasses onto the top of her head. "They were murdered."

At first Glory thought it was some kind of crude joke, but Leilani's frown was deadly serious. "What happened?"

"I don't know if you remember—a few years back there was an uprising by rebels in Russia. They took some hostages, did some damage. It took armed forces to quell it."

"I recall something about that."

"A school was bombed, and a little boy who was badly injured was flown here for treatment. His name was Sam." Leilani's voice dropped to a whisper. "I was here the day they brought him in with his father, Viktor. Sam's mother had been a teacher at the school, his siblings were students there. An entire family was gone—except for Sam and his dad."

A pang of loss for this man she'd never met rippled deep. Glory knew too well what it was like to lose loved ones.

"Diana, Dr. Steele's wife, felt Sam should be taken elsewhere, that he was too damaged for the grafting procedure."

"She was a doctor?"

"A pediatrician. Dr. Steele is the boss, but she was the oil that kept everything running smoothly." Leilani smiled. "In fact, you're doing her job."

Glory almost groaned. That explained Jared's attitude. She'd waltzed in and begun changing everything his dead wife had organized.

"Anyway, Diana wanted to transfer Sam somewhere else, but by then Dr. Steele had done the procedure many times with great success and felt he could help. He'd heard their story, you see, and it touched him. He understood Viktor was going through a father's worst nightmare. Jared desperately wanted to give Viktor back his son."

"So he did the procedure." A sense of dread hung in the air.

"It went perfectly. Two days later, Sam died."

"Oh, no."

"It was horrible." Leilani's voice dropped. "Jared couldn't understand it. There was no warning, no sign that the boy was in trouble. Even the autopsy couldn't explain why, only that his little heart had stopped."

"The father was devastated," she guessed.

"And furious."

"Oh?"

"Viktor agreed to bring Sam to Agapé because a doctor in Moscow had told him of our success. Viktor wasn't a religious man himself, but he thought his son would do better among those who believe in the power of God." Leilani pursed her lips. "You know how people are—get God on your side and you'll get a double benefit—less risk of anything going wrong if God's involved."

"I'm familiar with that line of thinking." Glory pieced together the sad story. "I'm guessing his view changed with Sam's death?"

"Yes. Viktor claimed Jared had talked him into it, said he would never have allowed his son to undergo the treatment if he'd known it was so dangerous." Leilani shook her head. "He'd been told all the risks. I was there, I heard it."

"The poor man. To lose that last link—" Sadness overwhelmed her.

"After the autopsy Viktor took Sam's body back to Russia to be buried. Before he left he threatened to make Jared pay for killing his son. It was an awful time. We'd all fallen for the little sprite, you see. Sam was a heartbreaker. We prayed so hard for him to be whole again." A tear trembled on her lashes.

"It's hard to understand sometimes, isn't it?"

"Yes." Leilani sighed. "But nobody took it harder than Jared. He locked himself in his office, reviewed the tapes of the surgery over and over, searching for something he'd done wrong. Only there wasn't anything. I should know—I assisted him. It was a straightforward surgery. It was difficult, yes, but no more so than others we'd done."

"Those are the hardest cases to deal with—the ones where you can't figure out how you could have prevented it. Or accept that you couldn't."

Leilani's sad eyes brimmed with tears.

"Diana and Nicholas were traveling home from a visit with her parents a month later. Have you met Kahlia and Pono yet?"

Glory shook her head.

"Lovely people. They adored Diana and the baby. And Jared. Typical Hawaiian family, lots of hugging, plenty of celebrations. They always included our staff in any party they threw. We'd become part of their family." Leilani blew her nose. "Diana's car went over the edge of a cliff. She and Nicholas were killed. After the funerals, Jared got a card. *An eye for an eye.* It was Viktor."

"How horrible!" Glory shuddered. "This Viktor—he's in jail now, right?"

"Yes." Leilani sighed. "Not that it makes any difference. They're still gone. I think Jared would have left Agapé, moved on and built a new life."

"Why can't he do that now?"

"If you haven't met them, I guess you couldn't understand." Leilani's troubled gaze met hers. "Pono and Kahlia won't let go. They cling to Jared as if he's their son. He finds it terribly difficult to say no to them, to add to the pain they've already endured. I think he feels guilty about little Sam's death, but he refuses to discuss it with anyone."

"But you said it wasn't his fault." Glory frowned. "This was when?"

"Coming up on three years."

"Her parents must be over the worst of it. He could leave now, couldn't he?"

"It would break their hearts, but I guess he could, if he made up his mind."

"You don't sound sure." Something wasn't quite right. "Why?"

"You should really talk to him."

"Dredge up his past without all the facts? How would that help?"

Leilani tucked her water bottle back into her bag, pulled down her sunglasses and rose. "We'd better get back."

"Wait." Glory held the woman's arm to stop her from leaving. "What aren't you saying?"

Leilani kept her mouth clamped closed, but a battle raged in her dark-brown eyes.

"You can't tell me this much and not the rest. It's not fair," GloryAnn pleaded.

"If I tell you, you'll leave." *Like the others* was the implication.

"No way. I'm not going anywhere. I promised Elizabeth Wisdom six months and that's how long I'm here for. So you might as well tell me. I'll find out, anyway."

"I guess you will." Leilani scuffled her toes against the dirt. Finally she lifted her head. "I think Jared doesn't leave because he can't. He often goes to Honolulu and visits the Halawa Correctional Facility to make sure Viktor's still there."

"Why?"

"I think he wants to make sure his wife and son's killer serves every bit of the time he was sentenced, be certain Viktor doesn't get early parole or something." Leilani shook her head. "Look, you really should talk to Jared about this. It's his private business, after all." She began walking quickly back to the mission.

GloryAnn remained still, the sun beating down on her head as she struggled to reconcile what she'd learned. An inkling of understanding seeped through.

Jared Steele kept a close check on Agapé to ensure nothing bad happened again. But why didn't he walk away, leave it to someone else, find a place where he could forget the horror that had happened here and move on?

If it took her entire six months, Glory was going to answer that question.

Chapter Three

Once she'd showered off the salty seawater and changed back into her work clothes, Glory hurried back to the wards.

The warm afternoons were the most difficult times for the children in Ward A, especially the older kids who couldn't yet get out of bed and move around. Technically she was on an extended lunch because she would be on duty all night, but since she had nothing else to do, Glory decided to help out.

The nurses hurried as fast as they could, but it wasn't possible to meet everyone's demands at once. The pathetic cries of those who had to wait for relief affected the others who watched in fear or studiously looked away to avoid seeing more pain.

Enough was too much. GloryAnn clapped her hands.

"Is there anyone who'd like to hear a story about a girl named Frizzy?"

"You don't have a book, Doc." Germaine, a preteen from the rougher side of New York, had been burned in an altercation between gangs and now used his bravado to bully his way through treatment. "How you gonna tell this story?"

"It's all up here, buddy," she told him, tapping her temple. Germaine's role as leader was well established in the ward. She'd have to make sure his interest was captured or he'd ruin it for everybody. "Do you know anything about the Arctic, Germaine?"

"Yeah. It's cold." He laughed uproariously at his own joke.

"Sometimes. Sometimes it's lovely and warm. Sometimes you can't see what kind of day it is because the wind whips the snow around so you're blind."

Glory kept describing the land she loved until a pin drop could be heard. Even the children that couldn't understand English well watched with wide-open eyes as she told a story about an Inuit girl, the basis for many Arctic folk tales. When she was six, Glory had changed the Inuit name to Frizzy so she could pronounce it more easily.

So caught up did she become in her story that she startled when a nurse touched her shoulder and pointed to the clock on the wall.

"Goodness! That's all for today. I've got to get some work done."

"But you didn't finish." Germaine's indignation echoed the others'.

"I'll tell you more tomorrow. If you behave." She shook her head at the calls for more, checked over a young girl whose pallor was worrisome, then hurried away to her office.

Unfortunately, Dr. Steele was already there.

"I'm sorry I'm late," she panted as she reached for

the first file. "Shall we begin with—" she checked the name "—Donald?"

That glacial glare told her he wasn't going to let it go.

"Dr. Cranbrook, we run on a tight schedule here. We cannot—"

Glory held up a hand. Jared blinked, obviously astounded by her interruption.

"Am I on some kind of time clock, Dr. Steele?"

He frowned, finally shook his head. "No, but it's important—"

"That I do my job the very best I can, which means in my own way, on my own timetable."

"Your point?" That jaw of steel didn't bend a millimeter.

"I'm not saying it's all right to be late," Glory hurried to clarify. "It isn't and I will try to do better. But it would be helpful if you didn't keep hounding me about every little thing. It's going to take me a while to orientate to your schedule but I promise I will fit in. Okay?"

Breathless at her own impudence, she waited for his acquiescence. His cold hard glare memorized every detail of her face, but he finally inclined his head.

"Thank you," she whispered.

"Donald will be discharged next week. Also these three," he said, indicating the appropriate files. "These four will be at least another month. The rest I am not sure about." He went through each case, precisely detailing the problems, what he expected and what he wanted to see before they were released.

"Are any of them candidates for your procedure, Doctor?"

"No." He rose, pulled his stethoscope from his pocket. "These will be the patients primarily in your care. If you'll excuse me, I have some things to do this afternoon away from the mission."

"I'm on my own?" she squeaked.

"Naturally not." He pulled open the door. "Dr. Xavier's at his cottage, on call. Dr. Potter's gastrointestinal upset seems to have abated. He claims he's feeling much better. He should be here in a half hour or so. I'll make sure he stops by to introduce himself. If an emergency arises, let the desk know. Leilani can always reach me."

"Oh. Okay, then."

Glory was talking to thin air. Dr. Steele was already halfway down the corridor. Whatever he had to do this afternoon must be important.

She spent the next few hours poring over every case, memorizing details she'd need if one of her patients took a turn for the worse. By the time Dr. Potter arrived Glory was twiddling her thumbs.

"Bored?" a lilting English voice inquired with just a hint of jollity.

"Well," she began, not wanting to say it.

"That's the problem with living in paradise." A salt-and-pepper head appeared in the doorway, lifted to reveal a sweetly rounded face wreathed in a smile. "As for me, I enjoy my free time by surfing, walking, sunning. I'm really just here to amuse myself until I retire. I'm Potter. Part-time anaesthesiologist, part-time attending doctor, full-time loafer."

"Dr. Potter, it's so nice to meet you." Glory accepted his hand then realized she towered over him. But as she searched his faded blue eyes it didn't matter. He was a kindred spirit.

"And you, my dear, though I must say I never imagined Elizabeth would find someone so young. It will be like working with my granddaughter."

"I hope that won't be a problem?"

"Hardly. I look forward to seeing your lovely face each day." He skillfully plied her with questions, nodded as if satisfied by the answers. "Shall I give you an idea of how the place runs?"

"Would you? I've already made enough faux pas. I don't want Dr. Steele to chastise me yet again."

"So Jared's been laying down the law, has he? Well, we must expect that."

"Why must we?" Glory asked curiously.

Dr. Potter blinked, pulled out a pair of glasses and slid them on to study her more thoroughly. Glory had the distinct impression no one had ever questioned Jared Steele's leadership before. Not that she was, but still.

"Jared and his wife started the place, you know. Agapé has only been in operation for about seven years." He chuckled, offered her a peppermint and when she declined, popped it into his own mouth. "Dr. Steele is always in charge. And when he's not in charge, he still is."

"I see."

He picked up Joseph's chart, clicked his teeth at the notation she'd made.

"If there's a change in a patient's condition, be sure you tell Jared as soon as you next see him. He doesn't like to miss anything."

"A little obsessive, is he?" she teased.

"It's not ego," Dr. Potter assured her. "Jared genuinely wants the very best for every child that comes to Agapé and he won't tolerate skimping on treatments or easing off just because it's painful." He shook his head, a rueful smile stretching his mouth. "I don't think I've ever known anyone quite like him. It's as if he's got a personal stake in every child."

Talk about setting yourself up for burnout. But Glory didn't say it aloud. Instead she thanked Dr. Potter for the information, promised to meet him in the cafeteria for dinner and agreed to look at a patient he'd been tracking.

"Dr. Steele mentioned he would be away from the mission this afternoon."

"Yes, he would be." A sad look flitted across Dr. Potter's sunburned cheeks.

"Do you have any idea when he might return?"

"I wouldn't dare ask." He rose. "If you'll excuse me, I must see if those lab results I was waiting for have come in. I hope you enjoy your time here, Dr. Cranbrook."

"I will if you promise to call me Glory."

He nodded. "And I'm Fredrick."

Glory sat behind her desk feeling much like a goldfish in a bowl as she stared through the glass walls. No doubt the design was intended to allow maximum air and light into the building, but suddenly everything seemed so strange. She decided to send her friends back home a quick e-mail, but either service was sporadic or someone had forgotten to hook up her computer.

She walked to the nurses' station.

"Leilani, how can I send and receive e-mail?"

The capable nurse tut-tutted her frustration, picked up the phone and uttered some commands in a language Glory guessed to be Hawaiian.

"Sorry," she apologized a few moments later. "Tomas should have replaced that router ages ago. If I don't keep on him—"

"Don't worry. No rush."

"You must be on Hawaiian time now. Anything else I can help you with?"

"No. I'm going to see the kids for a while. The little ones."

"Your heart's with the babies, eh?" Leilani tut-tutted again. "Don't miss afternoon tea. It always tastes like nectar after you've soothed the *keiki*."

On Ward C, the tiniest children were fretful. Glory-Ann thought perhaps it was the heat. She lifted a fractious toddler from a nurse's overburdened arms. He felt too warm.

"Is the air-conditioning on?"

"Yes, Doctor. But we don't want to turn it too high. Three of them have a fever."

"Which three?" The culprits identified, Glory glanced around the room, made a decision. "Get some sheets, please."

The nurses obeyed though their faces displayed their skepticism. Glory spread the sheets on the floor in a corner away from the vents. She pulled two screens in to further cut off direct airflow. Then she removed all but the diaper from the eldest.

"Dr. Steele does not allow the children to play on the floor," the pediatric supervisor advised, her face disapproving.

"Are you questioning my treatment?" Glory asked softly.

They were loyal to Jared Steele and that was fine,

but Glory had to make her own position clear now, before there was an emergency that would demand immediate obedience.

"No, Doctor." Without another word the nurse undressed two other children and set them on the sheets. They immediately stopped crying and began to crawl.

With the help of a third nurse they used rattles and other toys as distractions to keep the children on the clean cloths.

"You see, he's much more settled when he isn't bundled up." Chubby fingers curled around hers as the golden-haired toddler pulled upright and crowed with delight. "Come on, darling. Take your first step."

GloryAnn played happily with the children for an hour, assessing their range of motion, the extent to which the burns impacted movement, and muscles they used as opposed to those they favored.

"It's nap time, Doctor."

She glanced up at the supervisor.

"Okay. I've seen what I need to." Glory brushed her lips against a tiny head before handing her patient to the nurse. "Ask Dr. Steele to check his heel when next he comes in, would you, please?"

"Yes, Doctor."

Glory stayed long enough to watch the nurses tenderly dress their charges. They fed each one then tucked them in for a nap. In less than five minutes there was only the creak of a rocking chair to break the silence of the ward, and that was made by a young woman. She sat next to a crib that housed a baby in a plastic-covered cubicle. According to Dr. Steele's notes, this seven-month-old girl had a poor prognosis for recovery.

GloryAnn paused beside the mother, whose eyes oozed unspeakable pain.

"We'll keep praying for her," Glory whispered. "She's God's daughter, too."

The mother's tremulous smile was better payment than a thousand thanks.

"A moment, Dr. Cranbrook."

Glory startled at the command. She straightened, preceded Dr. Steele from the ward.

"Oh, you're back," she blurted without thinking. "How was Honolulu?"

If anything, his face grew even grimmer.

"I was not in Honolulu," he snapped.

"Oh, sorry. I thought—" His gray face looked so forbidding Glory let the comment die. "Is there something special you need to speak to me about?"

"Babies." His austere face frosted in the glare of the overhead lights. "On the floor."

"It's not the usual practice, I admit, but it did get results." She inclined her head toward the glass wall separating them from the nursery. "They've gone to sleep nicely."

"Placing them on the floor is totally unsuitable, Dr. Cranbrook."

"Unsuitable? Because it doesn't benefit the child, in your opinion, or because it wasn't your idea?" She was sick of playing power games.

He drew himself to his full height, a muscle in his jaw flickered. Glory grasped his arm to stop whatever words with which he intended to censure her.

"Look, I know you don't like me. I've made too many changes, probably pushed too hard, too." She dared not stop. "But my method did work, the sheets had been sterilized and the kids are now comfortable."

He crossed his arms over his chest, said nothing.

"I'm just as concerned as you that they heal." Fully aware that she was giving away her nervousness by talking so fast, Glory pressed on. "To that end, I'd like to know where I could go to get a pool."

"A—what?"

His frown would have cowed most people. But Glory couldn't stop. She had to make him understand that she wouldn't run away or give up simply because he was in a bad humor. She was here to do her job and she would do it no matter what.

"A pool. Where do I get one?"

"Are you mad?"

"Sometimes. But at the moment I'm perfectly serious."

"We are a mission funded entirely by Elizabeth Wisdom's foundation. We don't have the kind of cash it would take to put in a pool, but even if we—"

"Not that kind of pool." She choked off a nervous giggle. "I'm talking about a child's pool, the round plastic variety that we can fill with a couple of pails of water and let them splash in. The range of motion on the two babies with shoulder burns has lessened. The boy with the wound on the thigh favors his leg and the muscle tone shows it."

She thought his face relaxed a millimeter.

"You think that by splashing around in the water, they'll forget the pain, or at least shove it to the back of their minds?" Jared nodded thoughtfully. "It could work."

"I'd suggest the ocean but the salt would only aggravate the new skin."

"And there's no guarantee they wouldn't be compromised by whatever's in the water," he added thoughtfully. "Using bromide rather than chlorine would purify pool water but shouldn't exacerbate the wounds."

"Then we can get a pool?" Glory held her breath, excitement building inside. "When can we go to a store?"

Jared didn't answer. His blue eyes peered across the hospital as if he saw something she couldn't. When he eventually glanced her way, the icy hardness in his eyes had melted.

"You don't have to go to the city, Dr. Cranbrook. I believe I may know of one. I'll check into it, shall I?"

She nodded, delighted by his promise. "Thank you very much."

"I think that should be the other way around. Thank you for caring." The beginnings of a smile tilted the corners of his mouth. "I apologize for hounding you. The children, Agapé—they've become my life. I confess I am a little overprotective."

"Which isn't a bad thing."

While he was in such a good mood Glory decided to press her luck.

"Dominic, the cute little guy with the black curls?" She waited, to be sure he knew which child she referred to. "His heel needs grafting. Do you think he might be a candidate for your new procedure?"

His face darkened the way shutters blanked out the sun and the animation vanished.

"No." His fist clutched at the bottom of his white jacket.

"But he's healthy, would withstand surgery very well, I believe. Surely—"

"I no longer do the technique, Dr. Cranbrook."

Glory's jaw dropped. Her brain sent a plea Heavenward.

Oh, God, why have You brought me here?

"Dr. Cranbrook, you're not hearing what I'm saying."

The frustration of not being able to heal Philomena, who he cared for deeply, mixed with three long nights and very little sleep chewed at the leash Jared had imposed on himself. That combined with the racket coming from Ward B, carried by wind directly into his office, had contributed to a headache of gargantuan proportions.

"I heard everything you said, Dr. Steele." She grabbed his arm. "Can we please take this outside?"

It was not a request. He followed her out of the ward and down the hall. The children's song stopped for only a moment before one of the nurses picked up the melody and began again.

Jared winced at her grip. Glory wasn't taking no for an answer. He slowed down long enough to get a good look over his shoulder. The mess scattered around the room sent his blood pressure three points higher. He dug in his heels.

"What is going on in there, Doctor?"

"My name is Glory. Can't you ever call me by my first name?"

"It's not professional."

She glanced around as if they'd snuck out of school for the afternoon. "Guess what? There's no one out here to hear you."

He closed his eyes, forced back the incessant pounding and counted to ten. At first he'd assumed her upbeat personality would mellow the longer she was at Agapé. That had not been the case.

"We're making cards."

"Making cards?" He frowned. "Making cards for—"

"For the children to send to their parents or sisters or whomever they want." She pushed her hair off her glistening rosy cheeks. That faint sprinkle of perspiration gave her skin a dewy glow. Silver sparkles littered the bridge of her nose like Hollywood freckles.

Jared ordered his brain to concentrate on business.

"Why cards?"

"Some of the kids are really lonely. Most of them haven't seen their family for ages. They want to know what's happening and they want to tell them they're doing all right. I've contacted an aid agency that has promised to get the cards delivered and bring back any return mail for the kids. The only stipulation is that we must get it ready for their pickup by Friday."

"Do you think it's wise to get them thinking about their missing families?"

"I consider it essential," she told him, her spine straightening.

Glory always stood up for the kids. He liked that about her. She'd stick in her heels and refuse to be moved from her position if she thought her kids would benefit. She seemed to have no other motive for turning his hospital upside down.

"Look. Artie's, Charles's and Albert's infections could have been contagious. After I isolated them, I realized they missed having the others to talk to, to commiserate with. I got them busy writing messages to the others. They wrote back." She shrugged, the fragile bones of her narrow shoulders outlined in the delicate white blouse. "Things sort of mushroomed from there."

Jared smiled in spite of himself. That, more than anything, explained her personality. GloryAnn was contagious.

"Is something funny?"

He swallowed, forced himself not to pluck away the bright-red dot that perched to one side of her lips.

"Why does making cards entail so much noise?" he asked, knowing she'd have an answer ready. She always did.

"That kind of mushroomed, too." She grinned. "I'll get them to tone it down, I promise."

"Don't bother." Surprise flared as he admitted the truth. "Almost every child in the place that's well enough to sit up and take notice is begging me to move them into this ward. You've got me in a very awkward position."

"Sorry." She wasn't sorry at all. In fact, she looked very pleased with herself.

Jared reached out and pulled the paper airplane from her fingers.

"This is a card?"

Dr. Cranbrook blushed.

Jared found himself amazed by the wash of rose that bloomed in her cheeks, lending her the soft romantic look of a young girl, an innocent.

Because that's what she was, he suddenly realized. Despite her training, her experience, her knowledge, GloryAnn retained her sweetness. She was genuine. She didn't play games, didn't kowtow to him. She just accepted that what she was told was the truth and moved on from there, doing her best to make a difference.

She reached to take the plane from him. Big blobs of glue bubbled on the ends of her fingers, almost obliterating her clear glossy nails from sight.

"I might have gotten a little carried away."

Jared held on, studied the intricate folds of the airplane.

"Carried away—ah, a pun." His face itched from her wise-owl gaze. "Do I assume the entire ward will now suffer from the same infection?"

"Don't be ridiculous! The glass partition still keeps them apart. I wouldn't risk another child's health."

She hadn't expected him to tease. Or thought he didn't know how.

"I was kidding."

"Oh." She tilted her head to one side. "You don't mind?"

Mind? Did she think he was an ogre? Jared almost snorted at his own stupid question. What else was she supposed to think when he stomped around like a grouchy bear?

"Apparently we'll have to set up a bigger workshop so that any of the children who want to participate can do so after they complete their therapy."

It was called caving in and he didn't mind a bit.

"Great." Watching her grin was like watching the sun break through after a squall. All of a sudden the world seemed kinder, gentler.

"You didn't go for your swim today."

Now she'd know he'd kept track of her movements.

"I wanted to get those cards finished." She glanced at her hands, began picking at the glue globs. "Did you get a chance to look at the baby that came in—after your initial assessment, I mean?"

He nodded, more comfortable now that they'd switched to medical matters.

"Yes. I agree with you. She bears definite signs of vitamin B12 deficiency. The tests seem to show a lack of intrinsic factor. You've ordered B12 shots?"

"I have, but I'd prefer not to proceed with any other treatments that are too aggressive right now. She needs time to heal."

"Agreed. And the boy—what's his name?"

"Naphir?" She waited for his nod. "He's going to need several surgeries to correct that back problem. I don't know how wise it is to do much before treating that."

They spent several minutes discussing the problem cases. Upon reaching agreement, Glory glanced at the children, sighed.

"I better get back. I was hoping to do an assessment of young August while he made his card for his mother."

"An assessment? Why?" What had he missed in the surly teenager?

"The burn damage was confined to his right hand, correct?" Glory frowned. "But he doesn't use his left hand properly. I ran some tests but couldn't find an organic reason for it. I'm going to look informally."

"You're thinking it's something psychological?"

Glory shrugged. "In the absence of a physical reason, yes. I checked his records. His brother was killed trying to save him. I thought perhaps he might be dwelling on that in some way."

"The shrink comes tomorrow. Ask him to talk to the boy." He saw something flicker across her face. "What?"

"August is very intelligent. He also knows English quite well. I think he'll say and do all the right things, just to please us. He wants to go home badly." She peered at him through lashes he'd first thought artificial. "I think he faked some of the tests he was given at his last psychological review."

"Because he wants to go home?"

"Because he wants to be with his mother, to protect her in case something else bad happens."

Jared considered it. Replacing skin was much easier than following the contours of the human mind. Glory shifted and he noticed some emotion flutter across her clear skin.

"You want me to do something."

She didn't come out and say no, but he could read indecision all over her face.

"What is it?"

"Can you just talk to him? Nothing medical, no lectures. Just talking. Maybe man to man you might be able to find out what's bugging him."

"I guess I could give it a try, though I warn you, I'm not sure I'll be much help. Diana, my wife, always told me surgery was my forte and to stay out of human relations." Jared gulped, stunned by the personal admission.

He'd made it a tenet not to discuss his personal life. Ever.

But Glory seemed to notice nothing untoward. She simply shrugged her narrow shoulders, studying him as if she thought he had all the answers.

"Could you at least try?"

He could not ignore a patient, especially not when another doctor asked him for an opinion. "I suppose."

"When? Tonight?" Glory asked eagerly.

"I can't tonight. I have to see a friend."

"Oh."

"There's something else, isn't there?" She'd kept back something he should know about. "What is it?"

"I'm very worried about August's mental state." She bit on the fullness of her bottom lip. "It really would be great if you could find time to speak to him today."

Suicide. It was always a possibility with the older ones. Jared raked a hand through his hair. At least the headache was gone.

"I'll go now. I was going to have an early meal so I could avoid the cafeteria special tonight. *Kalo* is not my favorite and *limu* comes in a close second. I can have my sandwich later."

Glory's nose wrinkled up, loosening the glitter so it rolled to the end and tumbled off, landing on her collarbone. Jared stifled his laughter.

"What are *kalo* and *limu?*" Worry threaded the nuances of her question.

"Taro and seaweed. They usually prepare a traditional Hawaiian meal once or twice a week. Most of the others love it but I try to be otherwise engaged."

"I'll make you dinner. If you'll see August first."

"That's not necessary."

"No. But I like cooking. I appreciate the cafeteria but sometimes it's nice to have something plain. Though I do love the fruits and salads here. And the flowers." She reached out to brush her hand over red hibiscus blooms. "We don't have anything like this at home."

In that moment Glory looked a bit lost and Jared realized he'd left her to settle in without even bothering to be sure she was comfortable. He felt a poke of shame for his callous disregard.

"It won't be fancy but it will be good." Her quizzical smile flashed.

"I'll talk to August, Glory. You don't have to bribe me."

She burst into laughter that echoed across the compound in a sweet ring of delight, chasing away his regret. Suddenly he felt carefree.

"As if I would." She snatched the paper plane from him, sent it sailing through the air. "What time is good for you?"

"Six?" he guessed.

"Six it is." She dashed across the grass, caught the plane before an upcurrent could carry it away, then hurried back inside the building.

Jared followed at a slower pace, his mind busy with the replay of Dr. Cranbrook chasing a paper airplane. She was a confusing mix—a dedicated doctor, a woman determined to help a teen, a nurturer who came back to the mission twice this week to sit with a little boy to help him through the pain. And now a cook.

Maybe he'd send Elizabeth an e-mail to thank her. Then he could tell her she needed to visit Agapé again. Soon.

Before Philomena got worse.

Chapter Four

"Running late, he says."

Glory slapped her hand against the alarm so hard the clock tumbled onto the floor and kept ringing.

"First he's late. Then he's delayed. Then he finally realizes he can't make it—at eleven o'clock! If you ask me, Dr. Jared Steele can't make up his mind about a lot of things."

She was cranky and Glory knew it.

Cranky because she'd worked so hard to make the meal perfect, cranky because she thought she'd finally broken through his leave-me-alone mask, and cranky because she'd stayed up until very late cleaning after his nonappearance at her perfect dinner.

Glory barely had time to drag a brush through her hair before her pager summoned her to the mission. She scooted outside, heard the sound of helicopter blades thrumming the air and raced across the compound to the hospital. At least she'd be too busy to be cranky.

* * *

"Kahlia, I have to go. There's a flight coming in." Jared gently set down the phone, hoping she'd forgive him yet again for cutting her off.

He raced out of his cottage, met Glory sprinting across the grass.

"You look awful."

"Thanks so much. Your compliments are exactly what I needed to start my day." She jogged ahead of him into Agapé.

Jared jerked to a halt, surprised by her sharp response. But the helicopter came into view. He'd have to deal with Glory later. Another damaged child was arriving on their doorstep.

Glory and Leilani were already on the tarmac. As soon as the chopper door opened, Glory had her hand outstretched, waiting for the chart. For once Jared stood aside and let her work without comment.

She took a quick look.

"Clean room, stat," she ordered then glanced at him. "Okay?"

Jared nodded, trailed behind the stretcher into the treatment room and followed her snapped commands, assessing her.

"Hello, sweetheart." From the gentle loving tone anyone would have thought she was the child's mother. Her gaze meshed with the boy's terror-filled stare. "My name is Glory. I'm a doctor and I'm going to help you. What's your name?"

"Bennie," the parched lips breathed. "My shoulder hurts."

"I'm sorry."

The boy winced away from her outstretched hands. Glory paused, waited till he'd searched her face, found what he needed. Finally he settled back against the bed with a heavy sigh.

"Okay now? Is that all right?" She remained absolutely still until he nodded. "How old are you, Bennie?"

She kept Bennie busy answering questions, soothing and probing as she appraised his injuries with a light delicate touch. Her tender voice, the sweet glow of love blooming on her face poked at Jared's midsection.

Glory Cranbrook. Quintessential mother figure.

Her heart lay exposed in her green gaze. Jared tried to swallow, to warn her against getting too involved, to demand she move over and let him handle this. But his throat muscles weren't functioning properly.

Anyway, it was too late.

His new doctor had tumbled head over heels for her patient.

"We're almost done, honey." She laid the back of her hand against Bennie's cheek, smiled. "You've been so brave, darling. Can you be brave a little while longer while Dr. Jared takes a look at your shoulder?"

Bennie studied him so long Jared felt like a specimen under a microscope.

"He looks mad." The boy's coffee-toned eyes stretched wide with fear.

Time to step up to the plate.

"I am mad, Bennie." Jared waited, as she had, for permission to examine the wound. "I'm mad that someone did this to you. I'm mad that you have to hurt. But I'm not mad at you." He smiled. "Okay?"

"Is he the boss?" Bennie asked Glory.

She laughed, musical relief in the quiet room.

"Yes, he is, so don't get me into any trouble, okay?"

Bennie nodded, winced as he tried to move in the bed. "Am I going to die?"

"No, sweetie. You are not going to die." Glory lifted her head, met Jared's gaze with blazing defiance. "We're going to make you all better. With God's help."

Bennie's big eyes welled with tears. "God doesn't care about me."

"You're wrong. God cares about you very much."

Glory's assurance stunned Jared. She inclined her head, motioning the others to help move Bennie to a gurney. Then she walked down the hall by his side, still talking about God's love for children.

"It doesn't matter what happens, Bennie, God's love never changes. Never."

Jared shoved the door closed on her voice, drew off his gloves and reached for Bennie's chart. According to the report, Bennie's injuries had been caused by an incendiary device that had mistakenly hit his house and killed both Bennie's parents and his sister.

A sign of God's love?

"I hate this world." But the words exploded inside his head, unheard by the staff now restoring the room to order.

Another family destroyed because men had never learned to get along with each other.

"If ever there was a case for your procedure, Bennie's it."

Glory's voice shocked Jared out of his private torment. "No."

"But you have to! He'll be horribly scarred if you

don't." She grasped his arm, her green eyes flaring wide, bits of orange flame burning in their depths. "He's lost everyone. How can he hope to be adopted with scars like that?"

"Dr. Cranbrook—" He stopped, chagrined by the sound of his own pompous voice. He took her arm, drew her outside where the others wouldn't overhear them. "Glory, I won't operate on him."

"Because?" Her voice came out hard, cold and flat.

"Because there are other procedures, other ways to treat him."

"None that would give him the same quality of life." She studied him, boring into his soul with that piercing regard.

"You don't know that. We'll try several different options, see which works best." He forced himself to sound upbeat, hopeful.

"Aloha, Jared."

He'd never been as pleased to hear the sound of that voice as he was now, when he didn't want to answer Glory's questions.

"Kahlia. I don't think you've met Dr. GloryAnn Cranbrook. Glory, this is Kahlia."

In her usual fashion, the Hawaiian woman wrapped her arms around the slim doctor, her eyes glowing as richly as her chocolate-toned muumuu.

"Aloha, Glory. I am so happy to meet you."

"And I you." If she was uncomfortable with the hug, Glory gave no indication.

"Did you invite her to Pono's birthday, Jared?"

"He didn't, actually. When is it?" Glory smiled.

"That's what I'm trying to figure out. Jared won't commit." Kahlia winked at him.

"I'd really love to come but I have to consider Sister Phil." Jared hated using her as an excuse, but he didn't want to be part of another big family celebration.

"Ah, the dear sister. I wish I could do something for her."

"Why can't you?" Glory's brief glance secreted a question in the dark depths. "I don't know her, but Leilani said visitors cheer her up. Would you mind?"

"Of course not." Kahlia's round face beamed. "She's done so much for all of us, it would be the least I could do for her. When should I go?"

In a moment Glory had recruited a helper. Why didn't that surprise him?

"For so long I have felt unneeded, useless." Kahlia's body drooped as she stared at the floor. "Pono and I loved Diana, and when she and Nicky died—"

Glory flung an arm around her shoulder.

"But there are so many children here who could use a grandmother. Why can't you adopt them while they're here?"

"Really?" Kahlia peeked up through her lashes, begging. "You would not mind?"

Jared felt like a mean-spirited grouch.

"Of course I don't mind, Kahlia. I should have thought of it myself." At the very least Jared figured it would keep her busy enough to limit her meddling in his life.

"Then it's settled." Glory's radiant glow transformed everything around her. "I know you're busy planning the party, Kahlia, but if you have a minute, I'd like to introduce you to someone very special. His name is Bennie."

"I do have time. Will you come to Pono's party? With Jared?"

"Barring emergencies, I'll try." Glory glanced his way, one eyebrow uplifted in a question. "Jared?"

"I'll try, too. Only you must promise not to be offended at the gift we give Pono, Kahlia." Jared grinned, watched Glory's face. "I'm putting her in charge of choosing one."

"What?" Rose flooded Glory's smooth cheeks. "But I don't even know Pono."

"You don't seem to have a problem getting to know people."

She arched one eyebrow at his snipping tone.

"You will love my husband, Glory. Just as I do." Kahlia beamed. "And you must advise Jared about gifts, because he once gave me a turtle. An ugly turtle."

"It was a stool."

"It was a homely, ugly turtle." Kahlia chuckled at his indignant snort. "You need all the help you can get, son. Now let me meet Bennie, visit Phil and then get home. For so long the days have dragged. Now I have too much to do and not enough time to do it in. I love it."

"You can tell me more about this turtle. Coming, Jared?" Glory asked sweetly.

And watch Kahlia's face when she saw Bennie's likeness to Nicholas? No. Jared didn't need the reminder.

"You ladies go ahead. I have to make a phone call."

"As long as it's not to a turtle shop." Kahlia and Glory giggled like two conspirators, then hurried down the hall, chatting a mile a minute.

"They seem to get along." Leilani stood by his side, watching.

"Maybe a little too well. I might have created a

monster," he admitted. "Both of them seem determined to gang up on me."

Leilani opened her mouth as if to say something, thought better of it and clamped her lips together.

"What?"

"I have to get to work." She turned her back on him and walked away.

"Must be something in the water," he muttered as he strode toward his office. "Everyone's acting weird today."

Including him. He'd wasted ten minutes this morning wondering if Glory colored her hair or if the highlights were natural. And now that he was alone he couldn't quite banish the snapshot of that blazing look of love she'd lavished on their newest patient.

Time to concentrate on work.

But the image of beloved brown eyes he'd known for only three years stayed in his mind.

The man who'd extinguished Nicholas's life could not be allowed to escape his punishment. Not as long as Jared breathed.

He had to make another trip to Honolulu.

Soon.

Glory knew she was spending too much time with Bennie, but this child was different, special. He grabbed hold of her heart and she couldn't break free. Nor did she want to. So she sat by his bedside, waiting until the painkiller had taken full effect. She heaved a sigh of thanksgiving as his little chest lifted and settled in a rhythm much like the tides outside.

"You're a special boy, Bennie. I know you're here for a reason."

Glory pressed a kiss to his damp brow then hurried to the other wards to keep the promises she'd made. Soon after, Jared came surging through the doors of the makeshift craft room she'd commandeered, his cool blue eyes iced frostier than Penny Glacier when the summer sun tried to melt its ancient Arctic ice.

"What is going on here?"

She took the small drum Toby had constructed from a can and held on to it so she could hear. "I beg your pardon?"

"This is a hospital, not a rehearsal hall." He opened his mouth but the words seemed stuck in his esophagus as he took in the painted rocks stacked at the end of the room. His face tightened even more, if that was possible. He glared at her. "What is that?"

"A pile of stones."

"I'm well aware that they are stones. Exactly what is the pile doing here?"

"Just sitting." Her sarcasm wasn't helping his humor. *Sorry, Lord.*

"We are getting ready to build an inukshuk, Dr. Steele." He blinked. "A what?"

"An inukshuk—it's an Inuktitut word. Technically it means 'a likeness of a person,' but it's a stone landmark used as a milestone or directional marker by the Inuit."

Seeing his confusion hadn't lifted, she launched into an explanation to buy time for his temper to mellow.

"The Arctic Circle has very few natural landmarks, so the Inuit build their own to mark a special ceremony or a date of significance. Then every time you go past it you remember."

"Very interesting, I'm sure." He rubbed his temple

with the pad of his index finger. "But this isn't the Arctic, Dr. Cranbrook."

So they were back to formalities again.

"No, it isn't, Dr. Steele. But it is a foreign place for most of these kids."

"Uh-huh." He shifted from one foot to the other. Waiting.

"The hospital is strange, we're strangers, and for most of the kids the palm trees, the ocean, the hills— none of it's familiar. They're strangers in a strange land, and they hurt." She tried to make him understand. "They need to do this."

"Because?" He glanced around as if bewildered.

"Because they need to have one thing in this place that is uniquely theirs, one thing they helped create. The inukshuk will be that, a monument that says to the world, 'I was here. I survived.'"

"It's a great idea, Dr. Steele." Nurse Kemper stepped forward, her eyes shining in her gaunt face. "The children are so excited. Some have even begun to discuss returning to Agapé after they've healed, just to see their stone. They encourage each other through the treatments. It's really exciting to watch."

"This one is Bennie's." She knew the moment she held out the hunk of black lava rock that he didn't approve.

"I see. And the drum?" He raised one eyebrow.

Glory giggled.

"That was improvisation. Toby isn't into painting. He can't write his name with his hands bandaged. Anyway, he doesn't know his letters yet. So he's making music for us to work by."

"Music. I see." A twinkle, the barest flash lightened

his steely eyes. "You really love these children, don't you, Doctor?"

The question disturbed her. If he had to ask— "Don't you?"

Jared never answered. His blue eyes fogged over in confusion as he studied the stones. When he paused at the exit, he studied her with unnerving intensity.

"I apologize for missing dinner last night. Perhaps I can make it up to you by treating you to lunch."

"That's not—"

"I'll meet you by the sea in half an hour, Glory. And bring your swimsuit."

"Yes, boss."

He glanced over one shoulder, as if to check whether she was taunting him, then left.

"Well!" Nurse Kemper blinked. "A lunch invitation. That must be a first."

"He's just trying to be kind. I invited him for dinner last night and he canceled."

"Yes." The nurse nodded. "I heard Sister Philomena had a bad turn."

"I must meet her, to thank her. She left tea and cookies with a note when I arrived."

Nurse Kemper's harsh face softened. "That's her. She's the sweetest thing. Agapé was originally her idea."

"I didn't know."

"Oh, yes. She's Elizabeth Wisdom's cousin. That's how Elizabeth became involved with Agapé."

"I'd like to meet the sister."

"She sometimes comes for tea, though I understand she's recently become quite frail." Nurse Kemper checked her watch. "I'd better get Toby ready for lunch."

Nurse and child hurried away, chattering a mad combination of English and a language Glory didn't recognize. She tidied the room, checked on Bennie, who was still asleep, then left the mission. It took only a few moments to change into her bathing suit, slip a beach dress overtop and grab her straw bag.

In her midsection, butterflies do-si-doed as Glory strolled down the path. But soon the pounding energy of the rolling surf washed away her tension. Excitement increased her gait. Somehow or other she was going to ask Jared the questions that lurked at the back of her mind and hope he answered them.

"You're late."

She jerked to a stop, startled by the sound of his voice. It came from below her. Glory kept walking until she arrived at the beach. Jared floated on the glassy smoothness of the sea, hands cupped behind his head, hair plastered against his skull.

"Come on in. The water's great." He dived beneath the azure sheen, skimming the bottom in strong motions that carried him a good distance out before he surfaced for breath.

"There's a reef out here if you want to snorkel," he called.

Glory nodded. She wasn't comfortable enough to risk going out so far yet, so she contented herself with paddling back and forth across the little cove while Jared cleaved through the water in a perfect front crawl, passing her repeatedly and mocking her caution.

Laughing too hard to properly control her breathing, Glory waited until Jared swam far out then she left the water. She wrapped herself in a big bath sheet and perched on the warm surface of a huge flat-topped rock.

"With your hair hanging around your shoulders like that, you could be mistaken for a mermaid beckoning a gullible sailor." Jared strode across the sand, breathing normally despite his exertions.

Glory couldn't help noticing his deep rich tan or the fact that he had the lean, honed shape of an athlete. After toweling off he pulled on a T-shirt, wrapped the towel around his waist and produced a big wicker basket, which he set between them before joining her on the rock.

"I hope you're hungry."

"Only starved." She licked her lips as he lifted out two plates of salad surrounded by a variety of crudités and cheese. "That looks perfect. Shall I say grace?"

He looked discomfited for only an instant before nodding. "Grace. Sure."

"Thank You, Father, for this delicious food. Bless the hands that prepared it, bless us as we enjoy it and let us be used by You. Amen."

"Amen." He waited until she'd tasted the first bite. "Okay?"

"Perfect." She munched happily away, enjoying the sharp bite of the dressing against the piquant flavor of the cheese. "I adore salads," she told him.

He snapped off the end of a carrot with teeth a dentist would love. "Why?"

"I guess it's because lettuce was never all that plentiful when I lived in the Arctic. Everything fresh has to be flown in and it costs the earth. It was a treat to have a salad. My mother would use every bit of produce, nothing went to waste."

They sat silent, enjoying their food and the glorious day. A pod of whales appeared in the distance.

"I wonder if they're the same kind we have at home."

"I've never been to the Arctic."

"It's beautiful."

"It's cold," he corrected.

Glory laughed. "Yes. But there are advantages."

"To freezing most of the year?" Jared made a face. "Name one."

It was the first time he'd been so carefree with her. His wrinkled T-shirt, a smudge of dirt on one shoulder, the mussed hair, the bit of dressing on his chin—all of it made him seem so human, so—touchable.

"No sunburn in the Arctic," she shot back.

"Not ever?" He chewed for a moment. "What about the famous midnight sun? That must cause some trouble."

"Well, yes, if you're silly enough to stay out in it too long. Which I'm not," she reminded as she let him take her plate. "Thank you. That was delicious."

"You're welcome. I have some coffee and pineapple, if you're interested. And some *haupia*."

"What is that?"

"Cold coconut-cream pudding made Hawaiian style."

"Yum. Yes, I am very interested." She waited till he'd served her. "Do you do this often?"

"Picnic by the sea?" He shook his head. "Not really."

"Why not?"

"When I first came here I used to, but I guess after a

while the thrill of living right next to the South Pacific kind of washed off."

"Washed off. Very funny." She leaned back to let the sun bathe her face, rested her back against another rock. "I don't think I could ever tire of this. I love the water."

"Did you go swimming in the Arctic? Is that even possible?"

"Most years we couldn't because the water around us was too deep and too cold. But there was a hot springs about ten miles away from our village. My dad drove me there a couple of times in the summer. It was gorgeous."

"Is that where you grew up?"

"My parents were missionaries to the Inuit. My mother felt Inuit mothers were the most skillful women she'd ever known. They taught her how to do their traditional handwork, to cook their way—everything."

"Is she there still?

Glory shook her head. "No. She died when I was ten."

"I'm sorry. And your father?"

"He loved to read. And they loved to hear him read to them. He's gone now, too."

"I'm sorry. I didn't mean to make you sad."

His quiet voice helped her regroup.

"It's all right. They're in Heaven now." She tasted a teaspoonful of the sweet dessert, savored it until she'd found enough nerve to say, "Can I ask you a question?"

"You can ask."

Meaning he wouldn't necessarily answer.

"One of the nurses told me Sister Philomena started the mission. That she's Elizabeth Wisdom's cousin."

"True." His face gave nothing away.

"She left me a carafe of tea and some cookies the night I arrived. I'd like to visit her, to thank her."

A shadow fluttered through his eyes. A small tic appeared at the side of his mouth.

"I'll be happy to take you to meet her another time, but today is out."

"Sure. No problem."

Dr. Steele had gone from an enjoyable companion to a block of ice in five seconds flat. Glory changed the conversation to something work related, but no matter what subject she touched on, she couldn't recapture their earlier camaraderie, nor could she suppress a certain awareness that there was something Jared wasn't saying.

A few minutes later his beeper went off and the interlude by the ocean was cut short before she could ask why he'd stopped grafting. They hurried back, slipped into their usual roles. Half the afternoon was gone before Glory realized she'd forgotten to thank him for the lunch, but when she had time to go looking, Jared Steele was nowhere to be found.

That evening for the third time in three days he was unavailable for a consult when patients arrived without warning. Glory and Dr. Potter struggled to handle two children in ICU with drug reactions. A host of other small but needy interruptions kept her moving as her workday stretched long into the night. She fell into bed at 4:00 a.m. for a couple of hours, then was summoned back to the mission, barely making it in time for rounds.

"Happy you could join us, Dr. Cranbrook."

"Dr. Steele, Dr. Cranbrook—"

"It doesn't matter, Leilani," she interrupted, stopping

the nurse's explanation of events from the night before. "Let's just get on with it."

"Finding it difficult to balance party time and work time, Dr. Cranbrook?"

Glory ignored Jared's snarky comment, though the same could be said about him. Apparently he'd had an even harder night than she had. His hair hung shaggy and mussed, a growth of beard shaded his jaw and his eyes were sunken and red-rimmed.

She cut him slack all through the day, but when he disappeared, leaving her on call again that evening, Glory was furious.

I'm losing my patience with him, Lord, she prayed silently as she checked a four-year-old for nasal infection. *Why am I here?*

As usual, the answer wasn't there. Frustrated, Glory pressed on, struggling to make her weary body keep giving. At three-thirty in the morning, after checking on Bennie for the third time, she took a break on the patio with one of the nurses, savoring the cooling breeze combined with the flavor of strong tea laced with thick cream.

"This shortage of staff is too hard on you doctors," the nurse murmured.

Glory nodded, tilted her head back and rested it against the chair and watched a spider climb up a pagoda-style landscape light.

"I hope Ms. Wisdom can find someone else soon. At this rate, you and Dr. Steele are going to get sick and there won't be anyone for the children. He's just like you— stubborn as a mule. Won't take even a moment off."

Glory frowned, sat up. Far out over the ocean lightning speared the water. The wind picked up, rustled the palm leaves surrounding them. Camellia blooms tumbled down, showering both of them in pink petals.

"At least Dr. Steele is home sleeping." Glory brushed the blossoms from her lap, took another sip of tea, hoping there was enough caffeine to keep her eyes open.

The nurse hooted with laughter.

"I wish he was sleeping. Then he'd be a little less difficult to get on with in the morning."

"Where is he, then?"

"With Sister Philomena."

"Oh. Visiting." That could hardly be as stressful as this.

"Sort of. She's just gone through her first round of chemo and she's not feeling very well. But then at eighty-seven, that's hardly surprising."

"She has cancer?"

The nurses nodded, her eyes sad.

"Dr. Steele noticed she was flagging last autumn, and when she wouldn't go to Honolulu for tests, he took her himself. We could hardly believe it when he told us. How could God let a sweet precious woman like that get cancer?"

"I don't know."

"Just doesn't seem right to me. Thank the Lord she's got Dr. Steele sitting by her bed through the night, caring for her."

So that's where he'd been.

"Couldn't she have a private nurse?"

"She could, I guess. If one would come. Nurses are in short supply in Hawaii, Dr. Cranbrook. Just like everywhere else. They can pick and choose where they want to work. Most don't choose an isolated place like this, even fewer choose an old woman in a shabby house with no money to pay them."

"Of course she's poor. I didn't think of that."

"She had some money to retire on, but Sister Phil gave every cent she ever got to keep this place going. I'm pretty sure Elizabeth and Dr. Steele chip in, though neither would mention it."

"I see." Glory remained outside after the other woman had left, pondering the situation as the wind cleared her mind. So Jared Steele was nursing Sister Philomena all night and trying to work a regular day, as well.

She had to do something. It was obvious things couldn't go on as they had. Everyone was overextended.

"Lord," she whispered. "Can You help us?"

No answer.

"I'll just sit here for a minute and wait for You to tell me what to do." She relaxed against the chair back so she could watch the black clouds scud across the sky, see the storm build over the white-capped water. What could a few minutes hurt?

Glory exhaled and let her tired muscles relax. Just for a minute.

"Dr. Cranbrook, may I ask what you're doing?"

Glory startled, blinked. Jared's face loomed above her, his mouth carved in a deep frown, eyes bloodshot, skin pasty.

"Dr. Steele. I was going to ask you the very same question."

Glory risked a quick look over his head to the far wall at the clock and suppressed her gasp. Six. Judging by the pink-tipped clouds, it had to be morning. She'd been bandaging a cut at 6:00 p.m., which meant someone had let her sleep out here all night. And her neck knew it.

"What question? What are you talking about?"

Every muscle in her body ached, her head throbbed and her mouth tasted like ashes mixed with raw liver.

GloryAnn was tired, fed up and way beyond cranky. She pointed to a chair.

"Sit down, Dr. Steele. You and I need to have a little talk."

He opened his mouth to protest, but she shook her head, clapped a hand around his arm and pulled hard. She met his glare with her own.

"You and I need to get some things straightened out, Jared." She used his first name deliberately, striving to achieve the forceful tone he used on everyone else. "This situation has gone from bad to worse. And it cannot continue. So I am instituting some changes, as of now. And I expect you to go along with every one of them—no, don't talk. Just listen."

He raised one eyebrow, crossed his arms over his chest and waited. Two staff stepped through the door with food trays, took one look and scurried away.

Jared plucked a leaf from her hair, almost ruining her moment.

"Well?"

"As of this moment you are relieved of duty, Dr. Steele."

"I'm what?" His jaw dropped in stunned consternation.

"Relieved of duty." She thrust out her chin. "As second in command, I have that authority. And I'm using it. You are in no fit state to treat anyone and you know it. Go home, go to bed for at least six hours. If you argue with me I'll be forced to go over your head."

"Really?"

The gauntlet was thrown. There was no way Glory could backtrack. She was a walking zombie, but at least she'd caught a few hours' rest. He looked like death warmed over.

"Yes, really." She looked him in the eye. "The board would back me if they learned the hours you've been working." He bristled at that, but she cut in before he could protest. "I understand you've been sitting with Sister Philomena. That's laudable, but you can't do that and continue your work here without someone suffering."

"Are you accusing me of negligence, Dr. Cranbrook?"

He surged to his feet, towered over her, marble jaw flexing as he controlled his temper. His eyes burned silver-blue with outrage, but something else lay hidden in the depths.

Glory shrugged off her nervousness. *Get this over with now.*

"I'm accusing you of working too hard. You've been harping about burnout ever since I arrived, Jared. It seems to me that you're well on your way to that yourself."

"I'm fine."

"No, you're not," she scoffed into his red-rimmed eyes. "But this is not a debate. Go home, go to sleep. At seven you're going to take the night shift here so the rest of us can get caught up."

"But—"

"I'll be making some changes in the scheduling, Jared. From now on *everyone* is going to take their days off as scheduled—with no exceptions."

He glared at her, thrust a hand through his hair. Finally he nodded.

"All right, I'll go. I'm too tired to do anything else. But if anything happens here—"

"If you show up in this building before seven this evening I will contact the board," she promised, ignoring the bulge of muscle in his forearm.

"You won't," he asserted, but a soft huff revealed his doubt.

"Try me. No one is indispensable. But each member of this team is necessary for us to function properly. We're already short two staff members. Dr. Xavier and Dr. Potter are doing their best, but we can't afford to lose another doctor. There are too many children counting on us—on you."

Indecision scribed a pattern over his face. And suddenly she understood.

"I'll find someone to stay with Sister Philomena tonight." Surely she sounded more confident than she felt? "You go home. Now."

His jaw worked for a moment. The tic returned to the corner of his mouth. But finally he wheeled around and strode to the door. He paused for an instant.

"Thank you." Jared disappeared.

Glory exhaled, sank onto a chair and counted the cost of what she'd just done.

"I have no clue how I'm going to accomplish this, Lord. There is no one to sit with Sister Philomena. Please don't let me mess this up. I couldn't bear to see his scorn."

After a quick tidy, she completed her rounds while questions ballooned.

Why had God brought her to Hawaii? And how was she supposed to help a man who refused to accept her help?

* * *

It was after eight the next morning before Glory left Agapé. Three flights during the night meant everyone was called back.

Instantly revived by the fresh air and the chirping birds, she stretched her legs in long strides toward home. Halfway there she paused, changed direction.

Today she intended to meet Sister Philomena.

As she approached a cottage that matched her own, Glory spotted a tiny figure clad in a flowered housedress bending over huge maroon hibiscus flowers.

"I'm fairly certain you're not supposed to be gardening." Glory smiled at the diminutive woman who faced her. "Last report, you were tucked up in bed."

"Don't believe everything you hear." The old lady's paper-white skin wrinkled in laughter lines.

"I'm GloryAnn Cranbrook, Sister Phil."

"My dear, it's lovely to meet you at last. Will you share a pot of tea with me in the garden? That way, when Jared checks, he won't see I disobeyed his orders."

Glory couldn't help smiling. She'd expected someone reticent and retiring, but this peppy woman with the snowy braids coiled round her head didn't fit the picture.

"Please sit, have some fruit. Since I've been ill, people have been flooding this place with fruit. I've sent enough over to Agapé to lower their produce bill for a month." Sister pointed to a plate of freshly trimmed pineapple spears. "Help yourself."

"Thank you. I'm still new enough on the island that this is like candy to me." Glory bit into the yellow sweetness. "We never had pineapple so sweet at home."

"Yes, I've heard you're from the Arctic. Tell me what it's like."

Glory heard herself go on and on. "Sorry. Guess I'm homesick."

"I understand." Sister Philomena stared out the big picture window toward the rippling sea. "I miss the change in seasons, but I can't imagine months of darkness."

"Have you been here a long time?"

They chatted until Glory noticed the older woman seemed to droop.

"I'd better get home." She quickly rinsed off the dishes, set them to dry. "Thank you for breakfast."

"You must stop in often, Glory. You are part of our family now." Sister's dark eyes twinkled. "Besides, I want regular reports on the children. Especially a little boy named Bennie."

"Did Jared tell you about him?" He hadn't seemed that interested in her favorite patient.

"Not Jared. Kahlia." Sister made a face. "Jared tells me all kinds of medical things, none of which helps me understand if I need to pray more for a child or move on. Jared's such a—doctor!"

Glory chuckled.

"Well, so am I, but I promise I'll try to keep you informed." She let herself gush about Bennie, thrilled that someone seemed to think he was as fantastic as she did. Finally she asked the one thing that bothered her most. "Sister Philomena, do you mind having people stay with you, other than Jared, I mean? I know you were expecting him last night, but when he couldn't come, Leilani suggested Kahlia. Was that a problem?"

"Of course not. I love visitors and Kahlia is one of the

best. She's just bursting with life, makes you feel better just to be around her. Rather like you, my dear. Besides, she's lonely. If I can help cure that, I'm delighted."

"Oh, good. I intend to come again, too, if you don't mind."

"I insist. But I mustn't be your primary concern. God has sent you here for a purpose, Glory. To fulfill it is your duty."

"Even if I'm not sure exactly what this purpose is? I mean, I thought I knew, but then Bennie came and Dr. Steele won't—" She didn't want to speak badly about Jared, so she stopped.

"Uncertainty is when we need His direction most, don't you think?" Sister rose, hugged her. "You will be in my prayers, child. I believe God has great plans for you."

"Thank you." As Glory walked over the diamond-studded dewy grass toward home, Glory felt cheered by her words.

All but the last ones.

God has great plans for you.

Did those plans include Bennie? And how did they involve Jared Steele?

Chapter Five

"Joy cometh in the morning."

Or, if not joy then energy.

Jared stood in the blazing sunshine and sipped the coffee he'd just made. For some reason the world looked brighter today. He'd adhered to Glory's schedule for a week now. Sooner or later he was going to have to admit she was right.

The telephone rang. He hurried inside to answer it, thinking of the clinic and how weary she'd looked last night when he arrived to take over.

"Yes?"

"Aloha, Jared. I hear in your voice that you are working too hard. It's a good thing I have planned a luau."

He almost groaned at Kahlia's cheerful voice. He'd hoped Glory had kept his former mother-in-law too busy to draw him into their family circle. Clearly not.

"A luau? What's the occasion?"

"Pono's birthday, of course." Her tone scolded him for not remembering. "It's tomorrow."

"I don't think I can make—"

"We hardly ever see you anymore, Jared. You missed Grandma's party."

The hint of reproach irritated but he struggled not to show it.

"I'm not sure I can get away tomorrow evening. I'm on night rotation right now." Jared shuffled through some papers he'd brought from the mission but couldn't see Glory's schedule among them. *At least I think I am.* "Can I check and let you know?"

"Of course. Bring Glory. Pono would be happy to meet her."

"I'm not sure Dr. Cranbrook—"

"Aloha, Jared, my son. See you tomorrow evening at seven." The phone clicked.

Jared set down the receiver, closed his eyes and tried to recapture his joy in the morning.

"Something wrong?" Glory waited in the open doorway.

"Not really."

"Then what—really?"

"Kahlia wants—" He cut himself off, started again. "Remember she talked about her husband's birthday. Pono's sixty-fifth birthday party is tomorrow night. She invited us to a luau."

"You don't want to go."

"No."

"So don't go."

If only it were that easy.

"The thing is, birthdays are a big deal with them." Any occasion was a big deal to Diana's parents. They lived life large, squeezed the joy out of every moment. Diana had been like that, too.

"So go." Glory leaned against the doorjamb studying him.

"Shouldn't you be working?" Anything to keep her from probing into his personal problems.

"Nope. And neither should you." Fun lurked in her green gaze. "We're off today. That's what I came to tell you. Or rather ask. I'm going to Honolulu. Want to come? You could look for a gift for the birthday boy."

"How were you planning on getting there?" he asked, holding up the coffeepot.

She shook her head.

"Well, if my powers of persuasion don't work on you, I guess I'm stuck taking the bus. Of course, the bus ride is very lo-o-ng." She stretched the word out, obviously intent on making him feel guilty.

It was working.

"The bus will take forever and I won't have time to visit Waikiki or Diamond Head or the International Marketplace or Pearl Harbor or the Arizona Memorial or—"

"Enough." He held up a hand. "You can't possibly see all that in one day, anyway. And why Waikiki? We have a far superior beach right here."

"Oh, Dr. Steele, it isn't the superiority of the beach I'm concerned about." She gave him that arch look, laughing at him. "Do you realize that it's January?"

"Uh-huh. Has been for about a month now." He finished his coffee, decided a third cup wasn't a good idea given that he hadn't eaten breakfast.

"At home it's the middle of winter—long dark days and bitterly cold weather." She pointed to her bare feet and purple-tinted toenails. "I want my picture taken under a palm tree with my toes in the surf at Waikiki."

"Just like any other tourist, huh?" He couldn't stop his laugh.

His calendar had a ton of notations. Forms due, reports overdue. Not the best time to goof off, but for once Jared didn't care.

"Okay, I'll take you to Waikiki and wherever else you want to go. But we'll have to leave right away. The road gets so crowded later we wouldn't make it back till late."

"Hmm. I'm ready." She lifted the straw bag she'd left outside his door and tossed him a cheeky grin. "How long will you be?"

"Conned again. It's getting to be a habit." He grabbed his suit, a beach towel and stuffed them into a bag. "Elizabeth should have warned us about you."

"Why?" She blinked innocently. "I've done everything you asked me to, the hospital is running smoothly and we deserve a day off."

Because he wanted to forget, because he was tired, because her bubbling delight always soothed his stormy mind, Jared would go and bask in the happiness that spilled over.

She was right. She had worked hard and she deserved to see more than Agapé's few acres while she was here.

He owed her that much.

"Sister Phil?" he asked as he backed out of his parking spot.

"Is well taken care of. If she needs help, Dr. Xavier promised he'd go."

"Do up your seat belt," he ordered.

But she'd beaten him to it.

The Hawaiian sun lived up to its reputation as they drove the winding road. Jared slid on his sunglasses, wondering if Glory preferred the roof up. Watching her nixed that idea.

Old ships bore carved mermaids on the bow. Glory resembled one now with her eyes closed, her thick golden lashes fanning over lightly tanned cheeks, nose thrust forward, hair streaming behind. She pushed her face into the wind as if daring it to push back.

Glory was well named.

"Stop staring at me." She didn't open her eyes or turn her head.

"Why? You look lovely. I believe you've even got a bit of a tan."

She did open her eyes then, her glare censorious.

"I have a lot of tan. For me, that is. And it's taken me ages to get it." She pushed her hand next to his arm and sighed. "It barely shows. I've poured on so much sunscreen, I should have bought shares. I'm sure they've gone up at least twenty percent."

Jared's tension blew away with his laughter.

"You should laugh more often. It gives you this handsome, who-cares attitude that women find very attractive. But then you probably knew that." Glory closed her eyes and resumed her pose. "How long will it take to get there?"

So she thought he was handsome. Considering his attitude toward her, Jared couldn't imagine why.

"We'll be there in less than an hour."

"Good. You'll have plenty of time to think about the gift you're going to buy. What does Pono like?"

Life. The big generous Hawaiian thrived on his family and friends and he lived each day as if he might not get a second chance to enjoy himself.

Unlike him.

"Jared?" Glory touched his fingers where they rested against the gearshift. "Did I say something wrong?"

"No." He fiddled with something on the dash to escape her touch. "Didn't Kahlia say *you* should buy the gift?"

"Hmm. What does Pono like to do?"

"He grows orchids, beautiful rare ones. He's been a member of the horticultural society for as long as I've known him."

"So flowers are out." Tiny lines fanned out across her forehead. "I'll think about it, but I'm not very good with conventional gifts. Though I do like shopping."

"You should have told me that before we left. I'm a terrible shopper. I once bought Diana a toaster for her birthday." He stopped, swallowed hard. *Not too bright, Steele. Like the lady wants to hear about your dead wife.*

Glory didn't seem to notice his gaffe.

"A toaster. Why?" Her jade eyes formed circles of curiosity.

"Because she almost killed herself trying to pry bread out of our old one. She nearly brained me with the new one."

A long pause followed his words. Jared stared straight ahead, wishing he'd never left Agapé's grounds.

"You must miss her very much. And your son. I wish I'd known them."

With those quiet words the awkwardness vanished and they returned to being coworkers on an afternoon outing. Relieved, Jared described the overgrown vegetation they passed.

"That's `ilima." He pointed to a bright-yellow flower.

"Used to be `ilima leis were for royalty. Over there are a bunch of ti plants, Asian imports that are very important to Hawaii."

"Because?" she prodded.

"The leaves make hula skirts."

She laughed but her glance shifted to the smooth white beaches.

"Want to stop?"

"Yes, I do. But no, I can't."

"Waikiki it is," he agreed. "You do know what the word means, don't you?"

She shook her head.

"Spouting water. Don't ask me why." He merged into the steady stream of traffic heading to the city's heart. "Finding a parking spot might take us a while. The sunseekers flood this place in winter."

"Ugh." Glory grimaced at the high-rises looming on either side of the freeway.

"They might not look like much but they cost a fortune. The price of land here is sky high."

"He jokes, too." She panned a droll look. "Where are you going?"

"Queen Kapiolani Park. It's right across from the beach. We can eat lunch in the park, hit the beach and visit the zoo without having to drive anywhere. And the International Marketplace is only a few blocks away."

"Sounds good. Look at the surfers. Ouch!" She winced, rubbed her side as if she'd taken the fall.

Jared found a spot and parked. A kids' band was playing at the band shell, so they traipsed over to listen. Glory dragged him to the war memorial, demanding he name all the flowers surrounding it. Next, she found a massive banyan tree and grabbed his hand to run it over the dangling roots with hers.

"What would you like to do next?" Jared asked.

"Shop for Pono's birthday gift." Glory shifted her bag to her other arm.

"It's too warm to lug that bag around. I'll lock it in the trunk and we'll come back when we get our suits later. Okay?"

She removed her wallet, handed over the bag. With everything secure, Jared led the way across the street.

He pulled her out of the way of a man dragging a huge shopping cart, threaded his fingers through hers. "Quite the nail polish, Doctor."

"I like purple." Glory glanced at their linked hands, then at him, one eyebrow tilted.

"It's easier to protect you. Just a block more to the International Marketplace."

She left her hand in his until they reached the famous outdoor shopping mall. Then Jared got caught up in Glory's wonder as she perused the assortment of T-shirts, muumuus, Hawaiian shirts and shell jewelry.

"It's wonderful!" She laughed, eyes sparkling in the shady alley.

He smiled as a hint of her fragrance, soft, feminine with an underlying hint of spice, captivated him. A moment later he shook his head when she held up a wooden caricature of King Kamehameha.

"No."

"Party pooper." Undeterred, she kept looking. "This?" She presented a T-shirt with a vivid orchid on the front.

"Um, I was thinking more—"

"Wait!" She turned the fabric to display a smart-aleck saying on the back, giggled when he rolled his eyes. "There's a fudge stand. You could get a nice big box to go with it."

When he didn't respond, Glory's face lost its glow of excitement. She folded the shirt and put it back.

"I guess tourist stuff isn't all that special for someone who lives here."

"Actually, the shirt's not a bad idea, as wrapping paper." Jared picked it up, suggested a price, then handed over his money to the vendor.

"Wrapping paper?"

"Your idea is a good one. Pono is mad about fudge, especially if it has Brazil nuts in it. I'll wrap one box in the shirt and order one to be delivered each month. Kahlia *claims* she's the best fudge maker around." Her hair was like a veil. Jared could watch it dance for hours.

"Is she?"

"Burns it every time."

"I get it." Her green eyes twinkled like sea diamonds. "This way Pono saves face."

"Exactly." Jared made the arrangements, then looked around to tell Glory he was ready to leave. He found her talking to a boy at a booth displaying kites. By the time he got there she carried a small bag and was paying for a massive blue bird kite painted in the Hawaiian style.

"It's bigger than you are."

"Isn't it great?" Her face was as excited as the boy selling it to her.

"You did barter, didn't you, Glory?"

"Of course not." She bristled with indignation. "I paid his price."

"Which was probably twice what he would have taken."

Jared sighed, shot the kid a glare. At least he had the grace to turn red. "They expect you to haggle, GloryAnn."

"I wouldn't dream of it." She leaned toward him, whispered, "He looks like he needs the money."

He shook his head, took her arm and walked her out of the avenue and back into the sun.

"You're thinking mad." She pulled her arm away.

"What?" Totally mystified by the comment, he waited for an explanation.

"It's what my dad used to say when I got angry but wouldn't talk about it. That's the way you look right now." Her chin lifted. "Thinking mad."

"I'm not mad, Glory." Time to make amends. Again. "Most of these vendors price their articles specifically so there's room to negotiate, and most of them enjoy bargaining with you. Don't forget they have a year-round built-in clientele of tourists."

"Oh."

He'd ruined it for her.

Jared chewed himself out, wishing he'd kept his mouth shut. He hunted for a way to coax back her joy.

"You're not going to fly that thing in the wards, are you?"

She giggled and it flooded back in a soft glow that lit her eyes and touched her lips.

"Of course not. I'm going to send it to my friend Kendra's son, Billy. He adores kites. Hey, that's a good idea. The kids could—" She stood still in the middle of the street, oblivious to the hordes jostling the massive package Jared now lugged.

"Come on, let's store this monster in the car. Then I'd like to have lunch."

"Great!" She looped her arm through his and trotted beside him, surveying the lazy shoppers, the street buskers and skateboarders with delight. "Can we go to a luau?"

"I don't think there are any noon luaus," he muttered. "Anyway, we're supposed to go to one tomorrow, remember?"

"Oh. Right." Her face fell.

"How about a picnic in the park instead?"

"Sounds good. But how will you keep that fudge from melting?"

He opened the trunk, showed her the cooler box he always kept inside.

She leaned one hip against the fender, crossed her arms over her chest and shook her head. "Dr. Steele, you are a man of many talents."

"I'm taking that as a compliment." He slammed the trunk shut. "I haven't been there in ages, but if nothing has changed there's a little place about a block over called Chow's. The best Chinese food you'll ever eat. Want to try?"

"Yes." She matched her stride to his. "Chinese food is my second favorite."

"What's the first?" Jared waited while she placed a dollar in a street mime's tip box.

GloryAnn winked at the mime, giggled when he winked back.

"I don't know what my favorite food is yet. I haven't tasted all the world's cuisines, so I can't be sure. But Chinese definitely ranks right up there. Oh, look."

Jared followed her pointing finger to a display window where a dress was pinned against a white background.

"Isn't it gorgeous?" she whispered, her nose mere millimeters from the glass.

It was. Swirling masses of variegated greens reminded Jared of the aftermath of a stormy sea. Sleeveless with a scooped neck, the dress fell in what Diana had once told him was a handkerchief hem.

"Why don't you try it on?"

"I don't really think it's me."

Jared looked from her to the dress and back.

"I think it's exactly you."

"Really?" A tiny smile flickered at the corners of her lips, a hint of yearning fluttering across her face. "I'm not really the glamorous type. Where would I wear it?"

"To dinner tonight." The words spilled out without thought.

"Oh. You didn't say anything about dinner. I didn't bring anything fancy." She worried her bottom lip.

"We won't have enough time to go back to Agapé to change," Jared encouraged, secretly amused by her hesitation. Her head was saying no but her heart was saying yes—and it was winning.

"It probably costs the earth. It looks like silk."

"You won't know until you go in and find out. Come on. I might just be able to hold off my hunger pangs long enough."

She preceded him in, eyes huge as she gazed at the beautiful clothes.

"Jared!" A dark-haired woman wrapped him in her arms then brushed her red lips against his cheek. "I haven't seen you for ages. How are you?"

"Fine." He had no idea who she was.

"You don't remember me. Diana introduced us at

your Christmas party a few years ago. We were school-mates."

Virginia? Veronica? He couldn't catch the memory.

"Vanessa," she supplied with a laugh. "And this is?"

"Dr. GloryAnn Cranbrook. She's with us at the clinic for six months."

"Welcome to Hawaii, Doctor. How can I help?"

From the corner of his eye Jared had seen Glory check the price tag of a nearby garment. She'd blanched and backed away. Now she apologized.

"I was just looking, actually."

"She wants to try on the green dress in the window."

"Of course. It will look perfect on you. One hundred per cent silk. Gorgeous fabric and cut. I don't know why I haven't been able to sell it, but that's why it's half off," Vanessa said as she lifted the dress out of the window.

Glory shot visual daggers at him, but the moment her fingers touched the dress she was hooked.

"I have a fitting room back here."

"You don't mind waiting?" she asked softly.

"Go ahead and try it on. We've got today off, remem-ber," Jared encouraged. It must have worked, because Glory headed for the back with Vanessa.

He sank onto a chair that was made for someone half his size and pretended he didn't look like a misfit. He couldn't remember the last time he'd come to town for anything other than business. He had, he now realized, become almost a recluse, visiting the city only when necessary to check on the man who'd killed his family.

After a few moments whispers emanated from the back room. He tried to listen in.

"You have to show him. You look beautiful."

"I'm sure Dr. Steele couldn't care less what this dress looks like on me."

"Come on, Glory. Jared would love to see this on you. Any man would. Don't be bashful," Vanessa said.

GloryAnn stepped out in front of him and Jared's breath stalled. She looked nothing like the doctor he'd grown used to seeing. This woman was a starlet. The skirt swirled about her ankles as she strode and pirouetted the way a model performs on a catwalk.

"Well?"

"It's lovely."

"Lovely?" Vanessa scoffed at his understatement. "It's amazing and perfect for her. Look how it changes her eyes."

He was looking. In fact, Jared couldn't look away. The dress—no, *Glory,* was stunning. A cross between a deep-sea mermaid and a forest nymph, with that long golden wash of hair she seemed ethereal.

"I'll never wear it once I go back north," Glory murmured, but it was clear from the way her fingers trailed over the silk that functionality was not a priority. She lifted her lids, met his stare and flushed before turning toward Vanessa. "I think I'll take it. Can we pick it up on our way back, in—" She looked to him, a question on her face. "How long will we be?"

"Ten minutes?" he suggested.

"Ten minutes," she repeated to Vanessa, who assured them she would have the dress packaged in tissue so it wouldn't wrinkle.

Once they left the store, Jared couldn't dislodge the image of Glory from his mind, let alone make conversation. So he simply kept walking.

"Um, Jared?"

He blinked at the tug on his arm. She'd stopped, was looking at him with an odd expression. He glanced up, saw Chow's sprawled across the canopy behind him in big red letters.

"Is this the place?"

"Yes. It's changed a bit." Pointless to hide his lack of attention. He could tell from that mischievous snicker that she knew he'd been daydreaming.

"It certainly smells delicious." Glory followed him in, gulped at the huge buffet. "Oh, my."

"Just choose what you like and they'll put it on one of those carry-out trays. They have lids so the food will keep hot till we get to the park." He watched as she wandered along, peering through the glass at each dish.

When Glory got to the end, she turned around and headed back toward him. The server behind the counter raised her eyebrows as if she couldn't understand the problem.

"Don't see anything you like?"

"Don't see anything I don't like," she corrected. "How can I choose? They all look scrumptious."

Thankfully it was too early for the lunch rush hour, so she had plenty of time to decide. Eventually he and Glory each chose a tray filled with different things they'd share.

"It's going to be way too much," she murmured once they'd picked up her dress and headed back toward the car. "And it's a good thing I tried on that dress first."

She cast a longing look over one shoulder at the store.

"Is something wrong?"

She didn't answer, reluctantly allowing him to put

her dress in the trunk. Jared pulled out two sea-grass mats. The park was across the street, but he hesitated before crossing the road. Judging by the way Glory was studying Vanessa's shop, something was wrong. He hoped she wouldn't ask to do more shopping.

"What's wrong?"

She looked at him, blinked. "Will you promise me something, Jared?"

"What?" Apprehension hovered.

"Do not let me go back into that store."

"Why?" Secretly delighted to find she had a weak spot, Jared spread the mats on the grass in the shade.

"I cannot afford it."

"Okay. I'll save you from yourself." He pointed to the mat.

Glory glared upward at the shading branches of the trees, held out her arm. "I thought maybe I'd get some sun today."

"Too hot now. Later." He handed her a plate. "What are you going to start with?"

Glory tasted it all but kept returning to the stir-fried veggies with almonds until she finally announced that dish was her favorite.

"Delicious." She leaned back against the tree trunk, surveyed the vista in front of them. "I can hardly believe I'm here, sitting right next to Diamond Head."

"Didn't you think you'd come to Hawaii or something?"

"I never thought about it. When you grow up in the North you don't really dream of something like this." She sipped her pineapple juice as she studied him. "What did you dream of when you were little?"

"Being a doctor," he admitted as he tidied up the mess. "I can't remember when I didn't want to be a doctor."

"How did you get interested in burns?"

He answered because they were still treading on safe ground.

"I did a round in emergency and found I had a knack for surgery. One thing led to another and—" he shrugged "—voilà."

"And your wife? Did Diana always want to be a doctor, too?"

Oddly enough it didn't hurt to talk about her. Not here, where the memories were in the past, bittersweet but not painful.

"Diana took her nursing degree first then went back and pushed her way into med school. Once she made up her mind, she never took no for an answer." He smiled at the memories. "She'd stomp all over your toes to get what she wanted, if she had to. Usually she didn't have to."

"Why?"

"She had a way with words. She came by it honestly. Her mother's the same. Kahlia won't be talked out of anything. By anyone."

"Was Diana Kahlia and Pono's only child?"

So much for relaxation. "Yes."

"That must be hard for you."

"Why do you say that?" Her astuteness surprised him.

Glory laughed. "I'm an only child, Jared. I loved my parents dearly, but I was not blind to their, uh—obsessiveness about me."

"What was your childhood like?"

"Wonderfully happy, full of friends and discoveries and God."

"God?"

She nodded, smiled.

"My parents were missionaries, remember? Because it took a while for people to accept us, we learned to depend on God for everything." Her voice softened. "At first there was no church, so we had Sunday service in our home."

"Oh." He grimaced.

She laughed.

"Actually, it was great. People would come for miles around. Everybody brought something to eat. My mother would stack the dishes around the stove." She inhaled. "You can't imagine the aromas that filled our little house during the church service. We could hardly wait for dinner."

Jared tried to picture it, couldn't.

"After we'd eaten, the kids would go out to play while Dad led Bible study for the adults. Then we'd all gather again to finish the leftovers and sample desserts. After that, everybody would head home."

"Sounds like a party."

"That's exactly what it was, a big celebration to God." She smiled. "My parents gave me the wonderful gift of faith. It still seems like a party whenever I walk into church and hear the music. It's like I'm coming to His house for a celebration."

Jared sat up straight.

"You must miss not going to church. I'm sorry I never thought of that."

"I do go to church," she told him with a smile. "Almost every day, in fact."

He frowned. When had she left Agapé? How?

"Jared, look around. What do you see?"

"The ocean, trees, grass," he rattled off obediently.

"And they are all His creation. Close your eyes."

He obeyed, waited.

"Hear that?"

"You mean the dog?"

She chuckled and her breath brushed his cheek.

"That's not just a dog, it's praise for the Master. Hear the waves? That's the sound of His robe swishing past. Feel that?"

The faintest wind rearranged his hair.

"That's His breath, saying He loves us, that He's near, watching."

Jared couldn't keep his eyes closed any longer. He blinked at her, ready to argue.

The words died on his lips.

The depth of her faith lent GloryAnn an inner radiance. It wasn't that she was naive, that she didn't understand the work of evil in the world. It was that she'd moved beyond it, into a deeper, richer experience. One Jared wished he were part of.

"Wherever I am, that's where I praise Him, worship Him, talk to Him."

"I admire your faith." It was the best he could do.

"Admire. But don't share." She sipped her drink, watched him intently. "Why?"

"I can't see God like that."

"Because?" She didn't seem offended, only curious.

Jared did not want to discuss this, didn't want to rehash the past again—ever. But he couldn't very well tell her to mind her own business, not without ruining the bond they'd built today.

"It's a long story." Maybe she'd give up.

"I have nothing but time today." Another sip, then she set down the drink, crossed her slim ankles and waited. "Go ahead. I'd really like to know."

"When we came here I really only wanted one thing—to be able to help those awful cases medicine had always sidelined." Jared made a face. "That sounds pompous and probably very arrogant, but it's true. I was sick of the politics, of the jockeying for surgical time. You know what it's like in most hospitals."

"Yes, I do."

"So maybe you can appreciate that I felt I was wasting time with the meetings and the bureaucracy. Somebody better qualified than I could do all that stuff."

"Your mission was to operate." Glory picked up one of the fortune cookies and began nibbling at the edge. "Go on."

"Diana thrived on meetings." His stomach clutched at the cascade of memories. "At one of them she met Elizabeth and learned of Sister Phil's work here."

"Burned children, even back then?"

Jared shook his head. A ripple of fondness brought back snapshot recollections of the tiny woman and her immense courage.

"Sister Phil didn't care what was wrong with them. If she found someone who needed help she made sure they got it. She was a nursing sister in England years ago, so she had enough knowledge to treat wounds, that kind of thing. There was a doctor in the village she bullied into helping her. She can be a tartar if she wants."

Glory nodded.

"One thing led to another and Elizabeth offered me a clinic here, on the island. One that would be for burned children. She'd just come from Africa and she was gutted by the terrible suffering she'd seen there."

"So you and Diana moved here."

"Diana was eager to return home but I held off. I wanted to be sure I was in God's will. We decided to pray about it for three months. If things fell into place then I'd know that was God's blessing." Jared stared at his feet, the burn inside igniting the guilt.

"That was smart."

"Was it?" He swallowed, continued, "At the end of three months I was convinced Agapé was our destination. Elizabeth never had any doubts so she had everything waiting when we got here. I plunged into work and learned more with every procedure. I did the surgery many times and never had a problem."

"Until the little boy died."

He wondered who'd talked. But he knew the answer. Leilani had been Diana's best friend. She'd been devastated when Diana and Nicholas—

"Jared?" Glory's hand stroked his arm, the heat from her fingers welcoming against his suddenly icy skin. "You don't have to tell me. I know they were killed by the boy's father. I'm very sorry."

"So am I." He cleared his throat. "It was the last thing I expected. I've lost patients before. It wasn't that I didn't think I'd lose another."

"There was no sign that the child wouldn't make it?" Her fingers threaded between his as if she was trying to infuse her strength into him.

It was not working.

"He came through fine?"

"As good as any I'd treated. There was no reason

to suspect—" Jared exhaled heavily, closed his eyes and traveled back to that day on the same path he'd trod a thousand times before. "I didn't make a mistake, Glory. If I had, I'd say so if only to make sure it didn't happen again."

"I know that, Jared. You don't have to tell me."

The warmth of her trust chased away the shadows.

"I've gone over the tapes, the records, everything, a hundred times. We record the procedures, you see. There's no indication that Sam wasn't recovering."

"Record—for insurance?" she asked, her brows drawing together.

Jared drew his hand from hers, instantly regretting the break in contact. Now he felt alone, abandoned. Which was silly. He'd been alone for three years now, ever since a madman had stolen his loved ones.

Ever since God let it happen.

"We record for learning, for teaching, so no mistake is ever repeated."

"But you didn't make a mistake." There was that confidence again.

"If I did, I can't find it. Nor could the panel that cleared me."

"So—"

"My exoneration wasn't much comfort to Viktor."

"Jared, just because his son died doesn't mean it was your fault." She considered a nearby family. "We know a lot about the human body but we don't know everything. I—"

"It's not that." He cut her off, disinclined to hear the excuses. Inside his belly, rage burned so deep he was afraid he'd scorch her with it.

"Then…?"

He curled his fingers into the grass and hung on as the bitterness poured out.

"I came here to help. I thought it was God's leading. In fact I was sure it was." The harsh laugh irritated his throat. "I thought this was where Diana and I could reach the most kids, where we'd both be happy doing what we loved."

"And wasn't it?"

"For a while. Before I got her and my son killed. Before He let them die."

"Oh, Jared. God didn't—"

"Don't!"

He couldn't silence his rage. The stark pain blistering his soul couldn't be erased, even by surgery.

"Was that God's will? Was taking my son, my wife— was that what He asked of me for thinking I was so great I could actually make a difference?"

"You do make a difference."

"Really?" He laughed without mirth. "Then why doesn't it stop? Why do the kids keep coming? Can't God stop it, Glory? Or doesn't He want to?"

"Neither one makes for a very loving God, does it?"

Not the answer he'd expected. Jared frowned, waited.

"How do you resolve it?" he demanded when it seemed she'd become lost in some daydream. "Tell me your concept of God."

She shook her head, a dimple flashing.

"I don't have a *concept* of God." She shushed him with a warning finger across his lips. Her eyes blazed. "I can't understand God, Jared. If I did, He wouldn't be God. I don't know why Diana and Nicholas died. I don't understand what would drive a man to kill someone. I have no easy explanations about why it happened or how you are supposed to accept it. Those are questions only God can help you with."

Jared's shoulders drooped. Whether she admitted it or not, Glory was in the same boat as he was. She just hadn't admitted it to herself yet.

"You're going to have to ask God your questions, wait for His answers."

"Do you think I haven't?" He surged to his feet. "I've asked a million times. There's never any answer. And blind faith just doesn't cut it anymore."

Jared could tell by her flaring irises that Glory was going to debate it and Jared just wasn't up to that.

"I'll go get us some dessert." He scurried away before she could reply.

He needed space to get his emotions under control. He needed privacy to quash his anger. Most of all, he needed hope.

But what he really needed, GloryAnn couldn't give because Jared desperately craved reassurance that Diana and Nicholas hadn't given their lives on a whim of fate, for no reason.

It was the only hope he had left to cling to.

Chapter Six

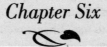

Will I ever learn when to be silent?

Glory's heart squeezed in pity as Jared marched across the grass, toward an ice-cream shop on the corner. A small boy on a skateboard crashed into him, but before the tyke could hit the ground, Jared had scooped him up and set him back on his feet.

Jared's devastating smile brought a like response from the child, who then hurtled off down the street toward a woman beckoning him. Jared watched him disappear into the crowd for several moments before he walked to the ice-cream counter.

He would make a wonderful father.

The thought shocked her until Glory realized it was true. When he forgot about the pain, when he relaxed and allowed himself to forget, Jared Steele was a different man. She'd seen that transformation repeatedly in the past weeks.

Did he cling to the anger to ensure he didn't forget his family?

"You're scowling. You don't like lemon ice?"

Glory blinked, focused on the clear plastic container in front of her nose. She accepted it dubiously.

"Lemon ice?"

"Take it from me, it's the best way to cool down on a hot day." Jared sat beside her, folded his long legs in front and began sampling his own treat as if nothing had happened. "How about a quick trip through the zoo when we're finished this? Then maybe we can hit the beach."

"Sounds good to me." She savored the cold sour bite as a parasailer floated across the sky. "That looks like fun."

"It is. Want to try?"

"Not in this lifetime. I'd probably crash into one of those high-rises or fall flat on my face in the water."

"I thought you liked water," he teased.

He'd left his sunglasses perched atop his head and the effect of that daring blue gaze boosted her heart rate. Why had she ever thought him cold?

"I like fish, too. But I don't intend to feed a shark." Glory tucked her hair behind her ear, too aware that things had changed between them.

She'd had no trouble keeping up her barriers until he let her peek behind the hard shell he usually presented to the world. Now she saw a grieving husband and father, recognized the thousand questions he couldn't answer. Only God could fill the hole that ripped him apart.

"Are you finished playing with that?" Jared quirked an eyebrow in the imperious yet fascinating way he had.

"It was lovely, but I'm as cool as I can get without needing a jacket."

"In Honolulu? Perish the thought." Jared lifted the dish from her fingers and tossed both in the trash. He slid the shades that hid his thoughts back into place. "Let's go check out the zoo."

The exhibits were fun, but Jared was even more so, as if he'd deliberately set himself the task of making her laugh, especially when he imitated the flamingos.

"They're amazing." The brilliant bird strutted across the grass. "Haughty and regal."

"They're actually white when they're newly hatched."

"They're so graceful." The brush of his arm against her side as he steered her away from a child's spill sent shivers up Glory's spine. "There are so many."

"Their colonies can number in the thousands."

"Look." She pointed to the sign, shifting away from his touch. "In Swahili they're called Heroes." To cover her fluttery nervousness when his stare intensified she began reading aloud.

Jared remained silent, apparently content to let her move from display to display like a fascinated tourist. Which she was.

"A Keiki zoo?" Glory dragged him into the flow of children.

"It's new. The fish tank in here is to hold people."

"That's appropriate." Only when he grinned did she notice she still had hold of his arm. Glory let go as if she'd been burned. "Sorry."

"You're as big a kid as the rest of them," he teased.

"Of course I am, but you knew that already. Oh!" A llama stretched its long neck toward her. Glory bumped against Jared's chest trying to avoid a wash by its tongue. "What a fantastic place for kids."

"A lot of the kids in Honolulu live in high-rises. This is like a visit to the farm for them."

She stood on tiptoe to watch children crawl through a tunnel to a glassed-off area. The kids ended up inside the fish tank, just as he'd said.

"Look at the color and size of those black koi fish," she whispered.

At the guinea-pig exhibit a little girl with glossy black hair stood rubbing her tear-filled eyes, frustrated by her inability to get to the tunnel where other children crowded.

"Isn't she sweet?"

Jared chuckled when the tiny girl swiped a hand across her face before bullying her way to the front of the line. She got into the tunnel with nary a backward glance.

"A woman who knows what she wants."

"That's one way to put it," Jared snorted. "I pity her dad. How could you ever say no to those big eyes?"

They stopped for a cup of coffee on one of the many picnic benches provided, then toured the Discovery Center, where Glory chose a video, some books and a few small toy fish for Bennie to play with.

While Jared studied the scientific journals, Glory chose a couple of brilliantly colored T-shirts for herself.

"You're not going to tell me those are for your friend's child, are you?" Amusement tinged his voice.

"These are for me," Glory admitted, slightly embarrassed. "Most of the things I brought aren't natural fabrics and I get too warm in them. These are all cotton."

"We could go to a mall. They'd probably be half the price."

"It's not the price," she told him with a glare. "It's the place. I'll be able to tell everyone I got them at the Honolulu Zoo. Everyone at home," she corrected quickly.

He shrugged, waited while she paid for the shirts. A

little breeze pushed in off the water and Glory was glad to let it cool her skin.

"Are you ready for a swim?"

"Uh-huh."

The size of the rollers breaking on shore made Glory apprehensive, but she didn't want Jared to know how afraid she was. So she walked with him to the car, retrieved her bag and followed him to the change rooms.

"I'll change and wait for you out here."

After pulling the long cotton cover she'd borrowed from Leilani over her swimsuit, Glory plaited her hair into a long thick braid and plastered on sunscreen. There was no other reason to hesitate from going outside, but she did.

"You like swimming," she lectured her reflection, glad no one else was using the facility. "You can manage to bob around for a few minutes."

It wasn't only the swimming. It was those piercing eyes and the way they made her mouth dry so she couldn't swallow. It was the timbre of his voice—

"Oh, grow up." She grabbed her bag and headed outside.

Jared tilted an eyebrow. "Ready?"

"I guess."

"It's a little rough. We won't go out too far until you get used to the surf." Jared led her past a grove of palms where the beach was wide with sand and a ton of sunbathers. He chose a spot, dropped his towel, kicked off his shoes then arched an eyebrow when she didn't move. "We can go farther down."

"What's farther down?"

"A seawall that shelters the beach on the other side

of that pier." Blue eyes gleamed innocence. "It's very calm there. The kiddies love it."

He was giving her an out, in case she was too much of a wimp to experience the surf. But this was Hawaii, and Glory had no intention of missing any of its delights.

"Maybe we could go there after. I'd like to try this first."

"Okay. Don't say I didn't warn you." Jared walked with her down to the water, rolled his eyes when she complained first about the scorching heat of the sand, then yelped about the water's cool temperature.

But he didn't splash or hurry her.

"It's lovely." The words left her lips seconds before a wave swamped her and she inhaled seawater. The strength of the surge tumbled her down to the coral-gravel bottom. Glory feared she'd never see daylight again until a strong brown hand grabbed her arm, drew her upward.

Jared waited while she coughed and spluttered her way back to reality.

"Don't turn your back on them," he advised, not quite laughing. "Try floating sideways. When the wave comes in it'll lift you up with the swell. Usually."

Glory tried it, found herself lifted and tossed toward shore.

"It's like riding a roller coaster." She winced at the bite of the seawater in her eyes. But that discomfort didn't stop her from paddling back out. She caught the next crest and laughed as it heaved her up and in toward shore. "I love this!"

"I can tell." Jared seemed unaffected by the ocean's strength. "Maybe you should try surfing."

"I have the balance of an elephant. I'd never be able to stand up."

"Actually, elephants have quite good balance. How about snorkeling?"

"I read about Hanauma Bay." How did he stay in one place so effortlessly? "A nature preserve, isn't it?"

Jared's expression left her curious.

"What's wrong with it?"

"Nothing's wrong but it's been over-visited for many years."

"Oh." Scratch that off her to-do list. He grasped her arm, turned her so a foam-topped breaker rolled harmlessly past, buoying them over the crest.

"That's not to say you shouldn't visit there."

"But you know a better place," she guessed. "Will you show me someday?"

"Sure."

Excited at the prospect of spending more time with him away from the hospital, Glory dived under to calm her pulse. Because of the rough tide, the misty water offered little visibility, but Glory poked at the coral bits anyway, crowed triumphantly when she surfaced with a small chunk.

"You're not going to keep that, are you?"

"Why not?"

He assumed his studious-professor look.

"Hawaii has a lot of coral. That's probably the worst specimen I've ever seen. Anyway, you're not supposed to take coral from the ocean. There are laws here, you know."

"Oh." Glory dropped it, watched it sink.

"The authorities would probably pay you to remove that one. But mostly we like our tourists to visit our stores and pay for their Hawaiian coral." He smirked when she used her toes to recover the prickly white hunk.

They splashed around in the waves until Jared called a halt, insisting they'd been in the water more than two hours. Glory disagreed until she got on shore and her wobbling knees testified to it. She was happy to relax with a shared plate of fresh pineapple spears after they changed. The shimmering water, the lush green of palms and spruce, the tanned bodies lying prone on the white sand and Jared's relaxed face all merged into a postcard she tucked away in her mind.

After the pineapple was gone, Glory strolled beside him on the beachside avenue, pausing every so often to read the signs as the sweet scent of coconut oil jumbled with seawater brine and white ginger. People rode brightly colored plastic trikes through the shallows, outrigger canoeists paddled parallel to the beach and white yachts cruised the aqua crystal water just far enough out to add to her shimmery daydream.

"This is lovely." Glory studied a stone waterfall with taps. Children and adults splashed under the spout, washing away the seawater and cooling down from the sun. Next to that a pergola-like structure perched just above the beach, one of several they'd passed. Beneath the open beams, tables with seats protected people from the heat. More benches faced seaward.

"Can we watch the sunset?" she begged.

"It's not the best—"

"Come on, Jared," she begged. "You can't be hungry again."

Annoyance crouched in his pupils, but he simply stepped back, waited for her to choose one of the benches. Two hundred feet out, the waves clashed with a concrete wall, spewing up white foam as it ran along the length like a giant tidal-wave fringe, a perfect frame for the end of the day and a fabulous show of nature. Glory sank onto the seat, her gaze riveted on the sky before her.

"It really is magnificent," she murmured as the last flamingo-pink rays flared once more across the azure sky before descending beneath the horizon. "We have lovely sunsets at home, but never at this time of year. That was fantastic."

"I guess it's a trade-off. You get the northern lights and they're pretty spectacular." Jared rose. "Shall we go?"

"I guess." Gas torches lining the street had been lit. Their dim glow enhanced the people now occupying the benches and picnic area around them.

"Let's get out of here." Jared took her arm, led her back onto the sidewalk by the street.

"Who are they?"

"Homeless." Jared studied them, a lingering sadness on his face. "They often use these shelters to sleep in."

"But the roof—there's no protection. What if it rains?"

"Then they'll find somewhere else."

At the other end of the area a man stretched out on a bench, swathed in a sleeping bag. Behind them a woman searched her shopping cart. Glory shivered.

Jared touched her chin with his fingertip, drew it up so he could look into her eyes.

"Don't be afraid. Mostly they're harmless, just looking for a place to sleep." He held out his hand and she took it, content to trust him as the night awakened.

In stark contrast to the dim pergola, people mingled happily in Waikiki's streets. Traditional Hawaiian music, jazz, even rock, floated from hidden speakers and fused in the gentle breeze. Fairy lights wound around palm trunks winked festively, while plumeria trees filled the evening with the sweet scent of their clustered flowers. Diners on patios above them tinkled glasses and china, their laughter floating down from balconies and terraces above the street, or sidewalk cafés.

A vendor handed Jared a pamphlet. While they chatted, Glory reveled in the aromas; coffee, barbecued pork, melting chocolate. Then Glory turned her focus to the faces; a man who disembarked from a tour bus, two teens, sunburned but laughing as they returned snorkel gear to a nearby shop, an older couple who held hands while they checked the menu board outside a restaurant fronted by huge bird of paradise flowers.

But she kept glancing back at the structure by the beach.

Why had it made Jared so sad?

"Two streets over they're serving fresh mahimahi. Hawaii's famous for it. Want to try?"

"Of course."

When they were seated at a table for two with frosty glasses of fruit punch, Glory asked Jared if he knew any of the people in the pergola.

"I used to." He leaned forward, elbows on the table as he rested his chin in his hands. "Nights are the worst time for them. I guess it's the same for a lot of us."

"What bothers you about the night?" A flash of surprise whisked across his face. Glory wondered if he'd tell her.

"I suppose it's the loneliness," he mused so softly she barely heard. "The feeling that you're all alone."

"You're not." She reached out, covered his hand with hers and held it for a moment. "You're never alone."

"God. Right." He turned his palm up, threaded his fingers through hers and smiled. But his eyes looked haunted.

"How did you get to know street people?"

"I went looking for Viktor after Diana and Nicholas died."

Jared's face grew taut, pale. She knew he needed to say more.

"Did you find him?"

"Yes."

"Tell me," she whispered.

"After the funerals—" He stopped, closed his eyes and inhaled several quick breaths. "After that I couldn't sleep. Every time I closed my eyes I'd see their bloodied faces, their frightened eyes begging me to help them." He sucked a breath in between his teeth, hanging on to control. "The police knew Viktor had done it but they couldn't find him."

"So you decided to help them."

"Not really." A sad smile tugged at his mouth. "Sister Phil forced me to take a weekend off. I couldn't stay at our house, didn't want to see Kahlia or Pono. So I drove here, visited the zoo. We'd taken Nicholas the day before it happened."

"Oh, Jared." Horror filled her. "Oh, I'm so sorry. I never—"

"Don't be sorry, Glory. He loved it there. I could almost hear his laugh today." Jared fell silent while the server brought their food.

Torn between needing to know more and not wanting to reopen old wounds, Glory picked at her fish. After a while Jared spoke again, his voice harsh.

"I must have walked for miles. Eventually I ended up sprawled on the beach, in front of that pergola. I was empty, totally empty. Or I thought I was."

Jared stabbed his fork into his fish and twisted the utensil, his eyes blazing.

"Just tell me," she begged.

"The tide came in, soaked me. I got up to leave. That's when I saw him, Viktor, sitting there, watching me." He laid down the fork, flattened his palm against the tabletop. "I pulled out my cell phone and dialed 911. He never moved, not the entire time. He just sat, staring at me."

His fingers curled, pulling the tablecloth into a knot as his hand fisted.

"I wanted to hurt him. I wanted to make him feel what I felt. But all I could hear was Nicholas's voice asking me where Sam had gone."

"They were friends?"

"They got to know each other when Diana brought our son to the ward one day. She had a meeting and I'd promised to take him swimming." His lids drooped over his eyes. "I looked at Viktor and I hated him more than I've hated anyone ever. I wanted to kill him but I couldn't move a muscle."

Glory had wanted to know more, but now she almost wished she'd stayed home today.

"They took Viktor into custody, tried him and found him guilty."

"But it wasn't enough for you." She could see the truth etched in his face, scribed in the lines fanning around his eyes.

"Of course not. How could it be?" He lifted tortured eyes to meet hers. "He stole my life, Glory. Everything I loved."

"And now he's paying for it." She nodded to the server to take their dishes. "Isn't that enough?"

Jared shook his head.

"Why?"

"No matter what you do, it can never make up for costing another person's life," he told her harshly. "I know that better than most."

Because of Sam.

"The worst of it is that the God I trusted, the One I served, let him do it." He pushed back from the table, bitterness blazing from his gaze. "Can we leave now?"

"Yes." Glory followed him from the restaurant, walked beside him back to the car.

Now that she knew the truth she was even more attracted to Jared Steele.

And there was no future in that. There couldn't be.

In a few months she'd leave paradise, and Jared, behind.

Why didn't Glory say anything?

As Jared drove the sea road back to Agapé, the scent of rain blew off the water. Palms swayed against the incoming breeze. Oncoming car lights pinpointed them like startled cats.

He felt drained, embarrassed, a fool.

Glory was adept at getting other people to talk. She'd appeared so interested that he'd been hooked, ended up spilling far more than he ever imagined he'd say.

He'd never intended to talk about his doubts in God, or about his torturous self-doubts. Yet Glory inspired confidences.

Quiet peace shone out from her eyes. He longed to experience that peace himself.

"What are you thinking about?" he asked, strung out by her silence.

"About what a wonderful day I've had. About my new dress. About bouncing around in those waves this afternoon."

"About Viktor and his son?"

She glanced sideways at him, nodded.

"You've all been so terribly hurt. Two homes broken. Two families torn apart."

Was that longing in her voice? But why? Her childhood had been rich, everyone at Agapé loved her. What did she know of losing your family?

A moment later Jared decided he'd imagined the inflection.

"I bought myself a floating bed while you were checking through the newspapers in that corner store."

"A floating bed?" That explained the huge bag in the trunk.

"A lounger. I'll blow it up and then float on the water, thus enhancing my tan and playing the part of mermaid. The Arctic mermaid. I'll make up a story for my grandchildren about my time in Hawaii."

"I didn't know you were considering marriage." The thought unsettled him.

"I'm not, not right now. But I'd like to be married sometime. Raise a family."

He could envision her daughter, a serious bit of a girl with big eyes that took in the entire world and left it better. Children made you better, richer, fulfilled. Glory would be a wonderful mother.

Grief at what he could never have clutched his heart. Jared shoved it away.

"How many do you want?"

"As many as my husband will let me have. Eight, ten."

"Brave man."

She grinned. "Or dumb. Kids cost money. But wouldn't it be an experience?"

"Yeah." Jared couldn't shake thoughts of Nicholas tonight.

"Oh, I'm so sorry." Her fingers touched his hand, squeezed it. "I didn't mean to be so thoughtless."

Would he ever get used to that touch, the whisper-soft brush of a sympathetic hand that expressed so much and asked so little? Did he want to?

"Don't be silly. Why shouldn't you talk about your future?" He pulled off into a beach area, rammed the gearshift into Park and opened his door. "Thought you might like to walk on the beach."

She didn't need a walk, he did. Away from her, away from the inviting scent of her perfume, away from the danger of thinking about possibilities. Children and family weren't for him. Not anymore.

"Shall I get the blanket? Do you want to sit on the beach?"

But Glory was already at the water's edge, dipping in her toes, edging a little deeper until the hems of her knee-length pants barely grazed the black-silk surface.

He watched her stroll back and forth, dousing her fingers in the water and tossing the droplets up to be tossed back on her, wet diamonds carried by the wind, landing on her cheeks.

"You want to go in, don't you?"

"I'd love to." Her winsome smile flashed. A huge breaker chased her out of the water. "But swimming at night is probably not the smartest thing to do."

"It's one of the best experiences you'll ever have," he murmured. "But I don't know this beach very well. It might be better to go somewhere familiar."

"It's probably past time to get back." GloryAnn strolled beside him, sandals dangling from her fingertips. She bent to examine a bit of driftwood the sea had discarded.

With the twilight around her, Glory reminded him of a traditional Hawaiian story about a water sprite that only emerged from the depths at night. He'd never seen anything more lovely.

When she stopped in front of him, he reached out, touched the moonlit-gilded strands that flowed over her shoulders and down her back. His eyes grazed past her smooth forehead, down her tip-tilted nose to her wide parted lips.

Jared brushed the smooth column of her neck with his fingertips.

And then his phone rang and the trance he'd fallen into shattered.

He flipped it open. "Yes?"

The voice on the other end was a newspaper friend he'd known for three years, and his words killed the moment.

"Are you sure? But why?"

The answer did not appease.

"Okay. Thanks for calling." Jared snapped the phone closed, squeezed his eyes tight and willed back the red tide of rage that threatened to consume him.

"Jared?" Glory touched his arm.

He opened his eyes, saw concern nestling in the corners of her jade gaze.

"Please tell me what's wrong. Who was that?"

"A friend."

"Is something wrong at Agapé?"

A laugh burst out of him, a sharp bark of mirthless rage. "Agapé's fine."

He wanted to go back to the sweet intensity of before. But Jared could no more keep silent than fish could stop swimming.

"He called to tell me that the parole board is meeting in a few weeks."

"P-parole board?" Glory blinked.

"Apparently some bleeding heart has decided that Viktor's mental condition makes him unsuitable for incarceration." He kicked his toe into the sand, watched the spray startle some nesting pigeons. "They want to release him to some kind of halfway house where he'll be under a psychiatrist's care."

"Maybe that's for the best," she whispered.

He shook off her touch, infuriated by the betrayal.

"No, Dr. Cranbrook, it is not for the best. The man killed two members of my family for revenge. He does not get to walk away without paying for his sins. I won't allow it."

"H-how can you stop it?"

The words snagged on his ragged nerves. He stomped around to her side of the car, yanked open the door and pointedly waited for her to get inside. But Glory didn't meekly obey his unspoken order.

Instead she leaned one hip against the metal and studied him.

"You hate him."

"Yes."

"You want him locked up, to suffer, with no help?"

"Yes." His jaw clenched.

"But hating him won't help. Hating him won't bring back Nicholas or Diana." She cupped her hand to the side of his face. "Forcing him to stay locked up instead of receiving treatment won't make you hurt any less." Her voice trembled. She inhaled, let her hand fall away. "Hating isn't the answer."

"It's the only thing I can do to get through the days and weeks without them."

"No, Jared." She pushed away from the fender. "It's the only thing you want to do. Hate is the easiest choice."

GloryAnn's soft words whisked past him on the night breeze, carried away by a rush of reality.

Jared recoiled as if Glory had shoved him. But she hadn't. She'd quietly taken her seat in the car, driftwood clutched in one hand.

He could almost pretend she hadn't said it—if he hadn't seen the pity in her eyes.

Chapter Seven

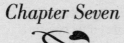

Two-twenty a.m.

The hours GloryAnn had spent in Honolulu with Jared yesterday seemed a distant memory as she sat by Sister Phil's bedside monitoring the slow rasping respiration. When the gnarled fingers lying in hers suddenly gripped, she began praying.

Sister Phil was not due for medication for another three hours. To increase it this early was not an option.

"Tell me what you and Jared did?"

Glory obliged by painting word pictures of the day, hoping to take the older woman's attention off her suffering.

"So in the end you never did get to wear your new dress." Sister Phil's sweet smile flickered to life. "Oh, well. You can wear it next time Jared takes you out."

"I don't think that will happen, Sister. I'm here to work." It was ridiculous how much she wanted another afternoon with him.

"He's a fine man, Glory. His heart is so big."

"I know."

"He thinks locking himself up here will make it easier to deal with his loss. But true healing only comes when you let go of the pain, reach beyond it to give of yourself."

Silence stretched. Glory leaned back, let her eyes droop closed.

"You could help him see past his anger, GloryAnn."

"No. I came to learn his grafting technique so I could practice it when I return home. Only, he won't do it anymore. Not since that little boy died."

"He blames himself." Sister accepted a sip of water then lay back against the pillow, her frail body too weary to hold her up. "He's lost so much."

Emotions had twisted Glory's heart ever since Jared had dropped her off at her cottage. Now they came pouring out.

"When he's not pushing himself to exhaustion, he's really fun. He loves the children, though he tries not to let them get behind his barriers. He works harder than anyone to make sure they get every opportunity they need, receive the best care he can give."

"But?"

"But I can't allow any personal feelings because in five months I'll leave here, return to the Arctic, as I promised I would. That's the calling God placed on my heart, why I have to focus on my patients."

Sister Phil fought her way through a coughing fit, proof that her lungs were not functioning optimally. "What else?"

"Rest," Glory ordered, worried by the pallor of her skin.

"No. Tell me—the rest."

"Bennie. He has no family but—I feel like I'm his family. Like he's my son. Isn't that silly?" Tears tumbled over her cheeks. Glory ignored them. "I tried to stay away, to be strictly professional when I'm with him, but I can't do it."

Glory pulled her bag near, tugged out the things she'd bought.

"Look. We were in the market yesterday and all I could think was, 'Bennie would love this. Wouldn't Bennie get a kick out of playing with this?'" She shook her head. "I was going to give them to him tonight. I actually considered waking him just to see his eyes light up. Isn't that crazy?"

"That's love."

"Of course I love him. But I can't adopt Bennie. Even if I had time to care for him, I'm leaving. Anyway, he needs Jared's procedure before he can fully heal. I'm already torn knowing I'll leave him behind, knowing I'll never see him or Jared again. How can I deal with that?"

Sister visibly gathered her strength. After several minutes she was able to speak, though only softly.

"God's calling is a very precious thing. Make very sure it's His voice you're following and not something else."

Sister closed her eyes, drifted off to sleep. Glory sat by her side as the pummel of waves rising and falling against the beach surrounded her. In the deepest recesses she heard her mother's voice, begging her to return to the Arctic and minister to the Inuit. The challenge was as clear today as it had been all those years ago.

Glory would go home, set up her practice and keep her promise.

God had not changed His call on her life.

As darkest night gave way to dawn, her mind spun scenarios from her day with Jared.

God hadn't changed his mind, but had she?

Jared paused in the doorway as Glory twirled in front of Bennie. The other children watched but it was Bennie's approval she craved.

"Pretty," he murmured as he reached out to touch her new dress.

"Thank you, darling." She laughed a sweet light trill of pure joy before brushing her lips against his cheek. "I'm glad you like it. I'm going to a party but I'll come and tuck you in when I return."

While a nurse urged the others into bed, Bennie stretched up one thin arm. The other was probably too sore from the wound on his shoulder. Jared shoved the guilty pang away, watched the child lean into Glory's hug, raise his chubby cheek for her kiss.

"Love you," the husky voice murmured.

"I love you, too, Bennie."

Anyone could see she did. Glory smiled, mossy-green eyes tender, her hand gentle as it brushed back his hair.

Though Jared had warned her many times, Glory had let herself grow too fond of this child. And that would mean trouble ahead. But for once, Jared didn't care. For once he simply wanted to relax and Pono's party offered the answer.

Glory tiptoed between the beds, her heels tapping against the floor despite her best efforts. She jerked to a halt when she saw him.

"Am I late?"

He shook his head, drew her from the room. "I'm early. And Bennie's right. You do look beautiful."

A rose-petal pink wash traveled up her throat at breakneck pace and suffused her face in a flush that only enhanced her beauty. "It's the dress."

Jared held her gaze. "It's you. Shall we go?"

"Yes."

She filled the drive to Pono's with meaningless chatter. Jared put it down to nervousness. He was experiencing a little of the same. Maybe it *was* the dress.

"This is the most beautiful front yard I've ever seen," she said as they reached their destination. "But since Pono loves to garden, I should have expected it to be."

Jared parked in the driveway because there was nowhere else on the street to park.

"It looks like the whole neighborhood is here," he muttered.

"Yes, it does." Glory shifted in her seat, as if she could hardly wait for him to open her door. The green silk hissed and rustled a reminder they were slightly late.

They walked together up the driveway. Jared placed his hand on the doorknob, then paused.

"You look very beautiful."

"You said that already."

"It was worth repeating." He twisted the knob, smiled at her surprise as the big koa-wood door swung in. "Nobody knocks at Kahlia's parties. She wouldn't expect it."

"Oh."

Maybe it should feel odd to take her to his in-laws' party, but Glory didn't look the least bit uncomfortable. She claimed that Kahlia's warmth and generosity of spirit reminded her of the Inuit back home. Jared introduced Glory to the birthday boy, who placed a gorgeous white lei around her neck, then enveloped her with the same warmth as his wife as he teased Jared about hiding such a beautiful woman at Agapé.

"Thank you for inviting me. I wish you many happy years, Pono."

"It is I who must thank you both for giving Kahlia a job." Pono leaned toward Jared. His brown eyes shone. "She's been so lonely. Helping out lifts her spirits."

"Credit Glory, Pono. I'm ashamed to say I didn't think of the idea," Jared admitted. "Dr. Cranbrook has been shaking up the place. I guess we all needed it."

Glory frowned as if unsure he was offering an endorsement of her approach or a criticism.

"I understand you grow orchids," she said. "I don't suppose you'd be able to help the kids with a small garden project, would you?"

Pono's face went from surprise to excitement in a second.

"I would be honored." Then a worried expression flitted across his face. "It's okay with you?" he asked, studying Jared.

"I would be delighted." Jared thought he'd schooled his expression quickly, but Glory's troubled look proclaimed otherwise. "She hasn't told me what the project is yet, but better you than me. You know how awful I am with plants."

"Yes, I do. You forget them and they die. I will come." Pono patted Glory's cheek. "Now go, find some food. Enjoy the luau."

The house brimmed with people who seemed surprised to see him there. Jared chatted with them, introduced Glory and watched the speculation begin. Same old, same old. A while later he steered Glory to the garden where Kahlia had a long buffet table stacked with delicious food.

"Is that—a pig?" Glory clutched his arm.

"Don't worry, it's not alive. Roast pig is a traditional luau favorite. They cook it in an underground pit."

"With the head on?" Her wrinkled nose showing her feelings.

"Yes." He lifted her fingers from his sleeve, snuggled them in his hand. "Aren't you the woman who wanted to go to a luau? And didn't you, Dr. Cranbrook, remove a gecko from a table outside the cafeteria just this morning?"

"That was different."

"So is this." He set a plate in her hands. "Try some. I promise you'll like it."

She pointed to a big platter.

"*Mano.* Shark."

Glory shuddered, ignored his amusement and moved down the table toward the fruit. With their plates filled, they found two chairs and a secluded table near the rear of the garden. Tiki lights lit up the garden, flickering in the breeze so the shadows danced over the burgeoning orchids.

"It's beautiful." She closed her eyes and inhaled. "I can't believe I really live here. If only for six months."

He couldn't believe he'd come back to this house.

"What are you thinking about?" When he didn't answer, she leaned forward. "Please tell me."

"I was thinking of Nicholas. My son." He lifted his

shoulders, sighed. "He used to love jumping off that rock into the pool. You had to watch him every minute."

"Which wasn't a hardship." Glory's voice brimmed with yearning tenderness.

"No, it wasn't." He grimaced, pushed away his plate. "Sorry. I didn't mean to get maudlin."

"It's not maudlin to remember your loved ones. I often do it myself."

"Who do you remember?"

"My parents. My memories of my mom are fainter now, but I can still hear her voice telling me she loved me. I hope I'll never forget that." Kahlia interrupted, asking everyone to gather round while Pono opened his gifts.

"I do not need gifts when I have friends like these," he announced, but his wife would not be swayed.

None of the gifts were lavish or expensive but rather a teasing combination of pranks and puzzles that made everyone laugh, including the one Glory had helped Jared choose.

"Mahalo, all of you. This is a wonderful birthday. I am blessed to have so many friends." His speech was cut short by Kahlia's entrance. She bore a huge cake with many lit candles. "I cannot be so old," Pono complained.

Accompanied by the cheers of the group, he blew out the candles then began passing around pieces of the cake. He declared Kahlia the best baker he'd ever met.

"They seem very happy together." Glory's gaze dug past his facade. "You don't think it was a mistake to involve them at Agapé?"

"I think it was an inspired idea. Kahlia's been at a loss ever since Diana died. I'm ashamed to admit I've tried to push her away."

"Why?"

Jared sighed. "I guess I wanted to bury some of the pain. Her presence and her constant reference to them kept reminding me of what I'd lost. I would have moved away if it weren't for Viktor."

Glory frowned. Jared rushed to explain.

"Maybe it's a cop-out, but it would be so much easier to escape the memories and the reminders away from here. Kahlia phones me on their birthdays. We have to go to the cemetery and put flowers on Diana's grave, balloons on Nicholas's."

"I'm sure she means well."

"I know that. But it's meaningless. I don't need to go through the motions." A wash of bitterness hit hard. "Believe me, I'll never forget those dates."

He was still in love with his wife.

Glory gulped as the knowledge washed through her heart. She covered quickly when Kahlia and Pono begged them to stay after their other guests had departed. She smiled politely, answered questions and pretended nothing was wrong.

But it was a relief to finally get into the darkness of the car interior and leave.

"Do you mind if we stop by Sister Phil's for a minute? Her doctor prescribed new meds. I want to see how she's accepting them." Jared glanced at her before returning his attention to the road. "Besides, I'm sure she'd like to see you in your new dress."

"I don't mind stopping." Glory didn't know what else to say, couldn't think of another topic to while away the time, so she remained silent.

"Was it too much?" He pushed a CD into the player and leaned back as Handel's "Water Music" played in the background. "I know they can be pushy and—"

"They aren't pushy at all," she told him sincerely. "I enjoyed the party. I'm looking forward to seeing more of them at Agapé."

"Then what's wrong?"

She could hardly say she was surprised that he loved his wife. Jared suddenly pulled off the road.

"What are you doing?" she asked.

"Something's bothering you. I want to know what." He must have realized he sounded like a drill sergeant. "Please tell me."

Glory scrambled for a topic, something that would appease him, or better yet, get him back on the road. She did not want this intimacy.

"I'm worried about Bennie."

"Bennie?" He frowned. "He seemed fine earlier."

"Physically, for now, maybe. But what happens when he leaves?" This was something she could talk about. "Why can't you do the operation on him, Jared? There aren't any medical reasons he shouldn't do well in surgery."

"I told you, I don't do the procedure anymore."

"Yes, I heard you. I just can't believe you'd waste an opportunity to help a child. He doesn't have to remain physically scarred."

"Stop it." His voice brooked no argument. He revved the engine, veered back onto the road and took the turn to Sister Phil's. Once they pulled up in front of her little cottage he got out, opened Glory's door then took her arm when she stumbled over the uneven ground.

His touch burned her skin yet she loved it. Glory was glad when they reached the cottage and she could pull away. No doubt Jared noticed her reaction, but he pretended to ignore it, though a tightness appeared by his mouth that hadn't been there before.

Glory headed straight for Sister Phil's bed while Jared spoke to a former nurse whom Kahlia had asked to stay with the patient.

"How are you, Sister?"

"I feel much better seeing you all dressed up. You look lovely, GloryAnn. I hope Jared told you that."

"Yes, he did." Glory could feel the heat behind her, knew he was standing there listening. *Ignore him.* "We went to Pono's party. He's going to help me out with a project for the children. And Kahlia's helping in the wards." Feeling like a schoolgirl, Glory finally got a grip on her tongue and sat down.

"You're so good at drawing in others, my dear. It's a real talent. I can just imagine how it will aid you in your work in the Arctic when you return."

Glory steered the subject back to the party, described the many gifts Pono had received. Jared, restless in the background, kept checking his watch.

"Do you need to be somewhere?" she asked him when the nurse came with medication.

"A friend was going to call me tonight. At home."

"And you don't want to miss it." She rose, bent to kiss Sister Phil's paper-white cheek. "I'll be back," she promised.

The crepe-thin eyelids lifted for a second, then drifted closed again.

"She's asleep. Let's go," she whispered to Jared.

"I'm sorry if I rushed you," he apologized once they were back in the car. "But I really can't miss this call."

"A patient?" Curiosity burgeoned at the change that had come over him. His forehead furrowed, his mouth was tense and he gripped the wheel as if it were a lifeline.

"No."

He didn't want to tell her.

But he didn't have to. She knew.

"It's about Viktor, isn't it?"

"Yes." He steered the car up the long driveway, stopped in front of her house.

"So you want to forget the past, to move beyond it? You're thinking of moving?"

"Yes. But Elizabeth hasn't found anyone for the mission and I'm not sure Kahlia and Pono are ready for me to walk out of their lives just yet." Jared got out of the car.

"Baloney." Glory opened her own door, climbed out and slammed it closed, angrier than she'd been since the day she arrived.

"I really—"

"You don't lie to your patients, Jared. You don't lie to the nurses, you don't lie to me. Why do you lie to yourself?"

His eyebrows lifted. "I don't know what you mean."

"Don't you?"

She would regret being so blunt when morning arrived. But tonight, with the darkness to shield her, Glory felt brave as the truth burst out of her, as clear as the moon above.

"You're not staying at Agapé for Elizabeth or the children or for your in-laws," Glory told him. "You're staying because you haven't got the guts to leave, because it would mean you'd have to forget about your vendetta against a man so grief-stricken he lashed out. You're staying so you can deny him recovery."

"My family didn't recover," he snarled.

"Will making him suffer change that?"

Jared pinched his lips together.

"Is not operating on the children really because you think the procedure's unsafe? Or is it to protect yourself from adding more blame to the already immense load you're determined to haul around?"

"How dare you criticize me?" he yelled. "You have no idea what I've been through!"

"Haven't I?" She thought of her mother's death, of her father. A sad smile tugged at her mouth. "What I know is that you've come through, Jared. With God's help, you've managed to keep working, keep cherishing a few precious memories from the past."

"No thanks to Viktor."

"Don't tarnish the legacies of Diana and Nicholas by turning them into hate," she begged. "It will eat you up and eventually, inside, you'll be just like him."

Before he could argue she turned and walked away, closed the door to her cottage and hurried out to the garden where no one would hear her soft muffled sobs.

Oh, God, why am I here?

Chapter Eight

Jared avoided her for one full week.

But no matter where he tried to hide, Glory always found him. Even here in the lab where he'd deliberately locked himself in, she pounded on the door until he responded.

"Took you long enough." She noticed his petri dishes. "What are you doing?"

"Working. Is there something you need?" He moved in front of her, refusing to let her see his notes. "Well, Dr. Cranbrook?"

"We're not going back to that again, are we?" She laughed, her green eyes glinting teasing flickers. "Okay, okay." She held up one hand, obviously receiving the 'do not disturb' message he was sending. "I need a judge. Or rather we do."

She was such a contrary mix of joy and whimsy and temper and laughter. How did she manage to pack so much into such a small body?

"A judge? For what?"

"For judging, of course. Our contest. Come on." She grabbed his arm and tugged.

Jared followed. He'd caught whispers all week, heard the giggles behind his back, endured conversations that stopped dead when he walked into the room. The staff was up to something. Which was exactly why he'd chosen to work nights and bury himself in here during the day.

"You have to put this on." She handed him a polka-dot blindfold. "We want our judge without prejudice."

Jared couldn't tell if that was a dig. Glory walked him through the hospital corridors, which sounded oddly hollow, empty. He detected the smell of today's lunch and figured they were near the cafeteria.

"Okay, you have to stand here." Glory pushed and prodded until he was finally situated where she wanted. "Is everyone ready?"

"Who's everyone?" A few giggles burst out. Jared identified several of the staff as they hissed admonishments. Then his blindfold was whipped away.

"Ta-da!"

Jared blinked in the harsh sunlight, gaped at the once white wall of Agapé's north side.

It had been painted. Every square inch bore some color. To the left of the sliding cafeteria doors was an aquarium teeming with the most exotic fish he'd ever seen. Astonishing patterns decorated the backs of some while others swam through the water with mercifully plain scales. The effect was both whimsical and charming.

"Now look over here."

Jared scanned the right of the sliding doors. Also an undersea world, but this one teemed with children, some with fins, some with breathing apparatus, and some with funny legs or feet that could have been webbed. They were aquamarine, purple, spotted, starred. But not one child had scars.

"Well?" Glory prodded, her hand tucked into Bennie's. "Which side do you like the best, Judge?"

He blinked, stunned by what she'd created. Behind her he saw the children, eyes as big as saucers as they waited for his decision. Any child that was able to walk, limp, ride, be carried or slid on a bed was gathered behind him. Excitement didn't begin to cover the energy that rippled through the group. Even the staff shuffled nervously.

"Say something," Glory hissed.

He turned back to survey the work.

"Who is responsible for this?" he demanded sternly.

"Jared, please don't spoil it." Her fingers tightened on his arm, her face implored him.

"I want to know who did this. You?" he asked August.

"Some of it, yeah."

Everyone was holding their breath, doubt beginning to creep into the happy expressions. They were afraid of him. Dismay filled him as one staff member met another's glance with an 'I told you so' look.

"I did some of it, too." Leilani stepped forward.

"Me, too," admitted Bennie, but his fingers clung to Glory's.

"Which part did you do, Bennie?" Jared hunched down when the boy pointed to a black blob that could have been a sea urchin. "I see. And August?"

"There." August pointed to an angelfish.

"Mmm, hmm."

"Maybe we should take the kids inside now." Glory's voice wobbled, on the edge of tears.

Beautiful strong Glory.

"I thought you wanted me to judge." He smiled at her. "But I can't judge this. Both of these are fantastic. I award both sides first place. Congratulations to all of you on a very good job. Do we have prizes?"

The tension snapped like an overtaut fishing line. Everyone began speaking at once.

"Thank you." Glory's glowing smile made him feel like a hero.

"I'm not an ogre, you know."

"I do know, Jared. Now so do they." She indicated the group, busily pointing out their part in the work.

"Potter painted something?"

"He sketched out the right side, Leilani the left. Turns out they've been spending some off-hours together, painting."

"Really?"

She nodded, grinning at his disbelief. "Really."

A cook appeared in the doorway, nodded at Glory.

"Come on, everyone. Cake and ice cream for the winners. Which all of you are."

They hurried inside for their treat. Jared stood back and studied the murals, noting details he'd missed the first time. The art really was a wonderful addition to the rather plain building.

"Aren't you going to have some cake?" Glory asked. She was alone now.

"In a minute. This needs something," he told her. "Can you get me a can of black paint?"

"Jared, they worked so hard." Fear crowded out the joy he'd glimpsed earlier. "Please don't—"

He laid a finger over her lips to silence her. "Trust me?"

After several breathless minutes she finally nodded, disappeared. When she returned, she carried a small black paint pot and a brush.

"Here."

"Thanks." He pried open the pot, dipped the brush and began writing in the only open space he could find.

By the Keiki.

Then he replaced the lid, wrapped the brush in one of the napkins that had fluttered through the door.

"You didn't think I wasn't going to be part of it, did you?" he asked, delighted by the grin that lit up her face, surprised to realize how much her quiet thank-you meant.

Glory crept through the predawn shadows, careful to avoid the pebbled path as she skirted Jared's house. The dew soaking her toes was worth it if it kept her secret a little longer. He still didn't know she was sitting with Sister Phil so often and she had no intention of telling him. Not yet. Not until she'd found some of the answers her heart needed to know about Jared and God's will for her life. Jared didn't need to know her inner doubts.

If only I could figure out how to get extra nurses.

But though she'd prayed nonstop for the past few weeks, no answer had materialized. Kahlia found helpers and when they couldn't come, she devoted herself to the frail nun, precious hours Glory needed to rest. But even Kahlia was running low. This couldn't go on for much longer.

"Good morning, Sister." She'd known the old woman wouldn't be sleeping, even though the sun hadn't yet risen. "You look pretty in that gown."

Kahlia rose from the chair, hugged Glory then bent to kiss her patient.

"I'll see you later," she assured her before beckoning Glory outside the room. "She's been quiet but I can tell she's suffering. The medications don't seem to be working that well."

"It sometimes happens. I'll speak to Jared."

"I've arranged for several visitors today—old friends who are making a special trip. They haven't seen Sister Phil in a long time. They want to repay her kindness." Kahlia held out a sheet. "I hope it won't be too much for her."

"I think she'll rally," Glory assured her. "You are a true blessing."

Kahlia drove away, promising to return to Agapé in time for an afternoon session of Valentine-making. She'd made a fresh pot of coffee and Glory poured herself a cup before taking her place beside Sister's bed.

"What shall I read this morning?" she asked, leafing through the worn Bible that always sat on the nightstand. "Continue in Psalms?"

A slight nod confirmed her choice and she read from the hundred and fifth one, marveling as the woman's lips moved, reciting the words from memory.

"I love those words." The precious rasping voice whispered the words with awe. "A testament to God keeping his promises to His children. We doubt so often and yet He is always faithful. How is your relationship with Jared?"

The question came out of nowhere. Glory described the murals and his response.

"It was amazing." And it had left a warm afterglow around her heart.

"God is working His way through Jared's shell." Frail fingers reached out to grasp her own. "And you, have you found the answers you seek?"

Glory shook her head. She felt so guilty for unloading on a woman who was fighting for her life, but Sister made it easy.

"I love it here. I love the kids, I love the work, I love the ocean and the sun—"

"And Jared?" the old woman probed.

"I—I'm not sure."

"You are troubled by your promise."

She nodded.

"I have to go back. Only yesterday I received another note from my friends. The interim doctor has not stayed as long as they hoped. Now they're looking for someone to fill the spot until I can return. I feel guilty about coming here and I still don't know why I'm here."

"Our Lord understood you would be torn by your decision to help Elizabeth, so stop tormenting yourself. Do the best you can, enjoy your relationships and wait for God to show you His way. But—" She had to stop to catch her breath.

When the spasm passed, Glory eased her back against the pillows.

"Don't talk anymore," she begged. "Rest."

Sister dragged another breath into her fragile lungs. "Glory, don't confuse your devotion to your mother with God's way."

"You don't think God is telling me to go home?" she asked in confusion.

"I didn't say that." Sister closed her eyes for a minute to rebuild her strength. "We think we know God's will. We read our Bible, pick out a particular passage and think this is what God is trying to tell us. But we're afraid to wait for the assurance in our hearts that we are acting as He wishes."

"What if that assurance never comes?"

"He will lead us, Glory. Never doubt He will lead us."

A light tap on the outside door broke through the hush that filled the room. A moment later Jared stepped inside. He didn't seem surprised to see her there.

"Good morning, ladies. You two rise early."

"We're after the worm," Sister Phil joked, tilted her head for him to kiss her cheek. "How are you this morning, Jared?"

"Well. I brought you some breakfast." He turned, lifted a tray onto the bedside table. "Fresh croissants and some fruit. Do you feel up to eating?"

"Perhaps I will wait awhile." She gazed at him. "Glory tells me Bennie is slow at recovery."

"He's as well as can be expected." Jared shot her a glare that accused her of asking Sister to intervene for the little boy who tugged at her heartstrings.

"I have seen a picture. He is darling."

"He is a heartbreaker."

That noncommittal response irritated Glory into speech.

"He's a damaged child who needs treatment to allow him to return to normal life. Jared's procedure could give him that but he refuses to do it."

"Sister Phil doesn't need to witness our disagreements, Dr. Cranbrook."

"I am happy to mediate." But Sister's gaze held Jared's. "Your technique was so successful before. Why not give Bennie a chance?"

"I will not do the procedure again. Ever." He shot Glory a glower that promised later discussion. "I will not bring disrepute to this mission and I will not endanger another child needlessly."

"It's not needlessly," Glory burst out, but Sister waved a hand to silence her.

"We are a place of help," she reminded. "By clinging to your guilt you only hurt yourself."

The clench of Jared's jaw proved he was fighting his impulse to argue. Glory wished she'd never begun the discussion. Sister Phil looked paler, weaker. A soft moan escaped her and she closed her eyes against the pain.

Jared snatched a syringe with morphine and injected it. "Relax," he murmured. "It will kick in soon."

"You both have work to do," Sister murmured. "Go now. We'll discuss Bennie later."

Glory would have protested, but at that moment a woman walked into the room.

"Kahlia sent me," she whispered after a quick glance at the bed. "To watch over Sister Phil. I'm a retired nurse."

While Jared explained his orders, Glory left as quickly as she could. But she'd trod only a few steps away from the pretty little cottage before his fingers closed around her arm.

"What did you think you were doing, drawing her into our argument?" The gentle tones for Sister Phil were replaced by indignation. "She's a sick old woman. She doesn't need to arbitrate our differences."

"Bennie is an innocent child who doesn't deserve to pay

for someone else's mistake." She turned on him angrily. "Have you even noticed the changes in his shoulder?"

She didn't need to wait for his answer; she saw it in his eyes.

"A few more months and it will be too late to help him, Jared. He'll be left with a massive scar that will begin restricting the movement he has."

"Don't lecture me," he snapped. "He's another child, one of many who come to Agapé. I'm not God. I can't make everything better for all of them."

"But you can for him. Bennie is one child, true. All we can do is help one child at a time." She lowered her voice. "You could maximize his opportunities, change the way his future will unfold. That's within your power. I don't understand why you refuse to help."

"I don't understand why he's become so important to you." His eyes probed beyond her shrug. "Why Bennie, Glory?"

"Why not? Bennie could be my child. And if he were—if that little boy was mine, I would fight you every step of the way until you gave your very best to him. Until you did everything you were capable of doing to help."

"Why?"

"Because I love him. Because that's my job," she sputtered. "Because that's what people, adults, civilized human beings must do to remain humane."

"Now I'm not humane?" He opened his mouth to say something, closed it just as quickly. Then he turned and stormed away.

Too late, Glory realized her implication had hurt him. Shame suffused her heart. She scooted forward, jogging to keep up.

"I didn't mean that, Jared. I wasn't trying to say you hadn't already done a lot. It's just that Bennie is—"

"What? Special?" He stopped so quickly she bumped into him. "They're all special, Glory. Beautiful perfect children who had their whole lives stretching out before them until God let them get hurt."

"You blame God for their injuries?"

"Of course I blame Him. Why not? Who else has the power to stop it?" He froze.

They both glanced up at the sound of an approaching helicopter. Another flight. More injured kids.

"I do the best I can for each one, Glory, whether you think that or not."

"I know you do," she admitted.

"Even if Bennie had the procedure, there's no guarantee it would make him whole again. And there is the risk that he would be worse off than he is now. Remember the oath—first do no harm. I will not endanger his life on a chance. I can't. I'm sorry."

He reached out, brushed a strand of hair from her eyes then hurried away, to Agapé to treat the new cases.

Though she was officially off duty for another four hours, Glory followed him. If she wasn't needed, she'd go down to the beach and let the tides and prayer heal her heart's hurt.

A week later Jared listened to the phone just long enough to ensure he would get the answer he wanted.

"It will be expensive," the voice assured him.

"I don't care what it costs. I'll pay. Get them here as soon as you can."

He hung up with relief. Kahlia had done her best, but

now Sister Phil needed more than someone to sit with her. She needed round-the-clock nursing care and she refused to go to the hospital, away from the place she'd called home for so long. Daily her lungs weakened— which reminded him.

He typed an e-mail and sent it immediately to Elizabeth. He wasn't going to downplay the urgency of Sister Phil's condition.

He checked his messages, caught his breath at the first one.

Preliminary hearing on February 14.

Tomorrow. Nicholas's birthday.

The screen saver came on. His son's laughing face framed by a red heart fluttered into view. A familiar pain knifed its way through Jared's insides.

He should have replaced the image long ago, but somehow he couldn't bring himself to erase the picture, take the final irrevocable step of removing this last secret reminder of what he'd lost. He'd come to terms with the fact that he'd never watch his son grow up, drive a car, date a girl. He'd accepted that Diana was gone, that he was alone.

What he couldn't accept was the reason behind their deaths.

Why? That's all I want to know—why did they have to die like that?

From days long ago in a Sunday-school class he couldn't even remember, a memory verse flashed to mind. "My ways are not your ways."

"No kidding."

"Talking to yourself?" Glory's head appeared.

"Yes, I am." He sloughed off the misery, forced himself out of his funk. "And no, I don't like my own answers."

"Okay, then." Glory leaned against the jamb. "You look like you could use a hug."

He found the prospect especially attractive.

"Are you going to give me one?" he asked, hoping to get a blush out of her.

"Yep."

"Oh." He rose, held out his arms. "I'm ready."

"Here you go." She leaned over his desk just close enough to slap three crudely cutout hearts into his palm. "Three hugs. Bennie added a kiss on the top one, too."

Her giggles chased away the shadows, brought joy to the room. Surprised to feel a certain lightness in his heart, Jared studied what she'd given him.

"A kiss, huh?" He checked out the Valentine. "Bennie drools."

"It's from the bubble gum. My fault."

She didn't look the least bit apologetic. Jared pinned each one to his bulletin board then extended his hand for her to see the wet blobs of glue dotting his skin. Glory handed him a tissue.

"That's all I get from you?" he complained.

"You were expecting something—more?"

"Yes. My enthusiasm for Valentine's Day is somewhat diminished."

"Maybe your expectations are too high." Her pert look made him laugh.

"Apparently." It was so easy to have fun with her. "I'm going into Honolulu tomorrow. Want to come along for the ride?"

"Yes!" Her eyes danced with anticipation. Then she frowned. "No."

"I like your decisiveness. Are you taking a vote?"

She shook her head. "My night to sit with Sister Phil."

"My sources tell me you've been doing that a lot," he said, watching her flash of guilt. "I'm grateful, but you're not doing it tonight. Don't worry, she'll have someone. I just had a phone call about it."

"She needs full care now."

"I know." He stepped out from behind his desk, slung on a lab coat.

"You found a nurse?"

"Private nurses. Several of them."

Her eyes expanded, green irises darkening to the shade of a forest in twilight.

"How?"

"I am a man of many talents." He grasped her arm and led her out of the room, down the hall.

"Apparently." She frowned. "Where are we going?"

"To see a patient. I need your help."

"My help? This is a stellar day. Are you sure you feel all right?"

Better than he had in a while. And it had to do with her and the pleasure he found in her company, but Jared wasn't going to tell her so.

"I'm fine. It's Maria I want you to look at."

"I don't recall a patient named Maria."

"She came in before you came on. House fire. Eighteen months." Maybe if he could get her focus off Bennie—

"What's the problem?"

"Neither Xavier nor I can figure that out." Jared held open the door to the ward. "Physically she's come through as well as we could hope. We'll release her to her home hospital in a couple of weeks if she responds as I expect. But she presents with complications. I'm not sure what's underlying. That's why you're here."

Glory focused on the little girl, her examination thorough. She teased the child, cajoled her, tried to engage her in some play activity, but the tiny girl remained stoically unresponsive to all the toys, her blue eyes empty of expression.

"I don't suppose the mom came along?" she asked, finally handing the child back to the attending nurse.

Jared grimaced.

"Mom's also in hospital, burned trying to save Maria. She's not able to be released, so baby's here by herself."

"I see." Glory scanned the chart, paused to take in some detail. "I don't know. Yet. But I will figure it out," she promised, handing back the orders. "Now, I want you to look at someone for me."

"Okay." Jared walked beside her through the wards. Past days of quiet contemplation were mostly over thanks to the array of projects Glory kept lining up.

Apparently Agapé had reached the culmination of her Valentine-making project. He already knew that the kitchen was busy baking special treats for the occasion, which happened to be a Saturday, the one day of the week free of everything but the most necessary treatments. One reason the kids loved Saturdays. He paused to watch two children manipulate the beads they'd been given.

"Brings a whole new take to the theories on restoring dexterity," he murmured so only she could hear.

"Dr. Steele says you're doing a wonderful job," she

told the group, slanting him a look. "He'd love to have one of your creations, if you have time."

Animation skittered through the ranks as the school-age kids rushed to reassure him they'd create Valentines especially for his office walls.

Glory was giggling as they left and headed for the next ward.

"You took pleasure in doing that, didn't you?"

"Yes. It's so much fun to watch your face get that panicked look."

"I do not get panicked."

"Really?" She dragged him over to look into a mirror hanging above a sink. "What's that, then?"

"Scholarly contemplation," he shot back. Then Jared realized where they were going. His stomach sank. "Glory, I don't want—"

"Oh, hush." She almost flew over to the small boy struggling to paste a paper heart onto a paper plate and knelt beside him. "Hello, darling. Can I help?"

For the first time Jared was jealous of a child. She lavished affection on him, her hand constantly touching his face, brushing his head. Despite her actions, Jared couldn't help but notice the awkward way Bennie handled the glue bottle, keeping his arm at his side so as not to stress the muscles and pull on the corrugated skin that had begun to fuse together. Glory worked with him, coaxing him to try different methods that showed more clearly than words that Bennie needed grafts and soon.

Jared pulled out a small notebook and began writing notes for himself. She was right. Bennie would be a perfect subject. His skin tone was the kind that repaired well. The minor grafts Jared had already done seemed to heal cleanly. If he could only—

Stop!

He looked up, found Glory's gaze on him and knew he'd fallen into her trap, begun to imagine doing the surgery in spite of his oath never to try it again.

He opened his mouth to tell her no.

"Am I going to get better?"

The soft-voiced query made Jared gulp. No prevarication there. Just an honest question from a little boy who needed the truth.

In that moment he was struck again by Bennie's likeness to Nicholas. Same big questioning gaze, same dark hair that pushed away from his skull in disobedient tufts. Same lithe grace as he flopped down on the floor to hunt for the little red heart that had gotten away.

Hunkering down beside the child, Jared waited until the boy was seated on the chair again, and then brushed back the flop of hair that wouldn't stay out of Bennie's eyes.

"You're already getting better, aren't you?"

So solemnly the dark head nodded. "But my shoulder hurts sometimes."

"Yes, because your body is trying to get rid of the skin that isn't any good. It's making new skin so you won't hurt as much."

Not a great explanation but Bennie seemed to understand.

"Will it always hurt so much?" Innocent brown eyes waited for an answer Jared didn't have.

"I hope not."

Glory and the nurse were busy with another child, so Jared got the boy back to work on his project, then hurried away. The sight of that damaged shoulder haunted him so badly that after he'd checked with Leilani he locked himself in his lab to review his files on the last fatal graft he'd done. If he could only find—

But in his heart Jared knew there was nothing to be seen in the tapes, nothing wrong with the procedure he'd completed.

The problem was something else.

Something beyond his control.

Chapter Nine

"Sure you understand?" Jared asked the private nurse who'd arrived half an hour earlier, while it was still daylight.

"Yes, Doctor."

"Good. I'm going to visit with Sister Phil while she eats her dinner, so feel free to take a break for half an hour."

She nodded, left the room. Jared turned to his favorite patient, noted her pallor.

"So autocratic," Sister Phil teased. "The poor girl was shaking in her shoes."

"Good."

"Pretend all you like, Jared. I know you're a marshmallow inside."

"Especially for you." He sat down beside her bed, opened the thermos he'd brought and poured out two cups of strong rich coffee. One he laced with cream and sugar then handed it to her.

Sister Phil accepted the cup, closed her eyes and breathed in the aroma, a smile fluttering across her lips. "Oh, that's wonderful."

"I thought you asked me to bring that so you could drink it," he complained, lifting the cover from one of the plates he'd brought along. "Try some with this."

"Glory," she guessed, smiling at the fruit slices arranged in happy faces. "Did she decorate yours, too?"

He lifted the lid, showed her the carrot-curl hair, radish cheeks, olive eyes. Sister Philomena chuckled.

"She just can't help herself," she wheezed.

He slid her breathing apparatus into place.

"When she found out I was coming here for dinner with you, she insisted on packing everything herself. I'm not sure our cook appreciated her interference."

"Don't be silly. Glory will have charmed him as she does everyone."

"Yeah." He gave a laconic smile, knowing it was true. "How's Bennie?"

"You, too?" he asked.

"How can I help but fall in love with such an adorable boy?"

"You've seen him?" he asked, then felt foolish for asking such a silly question.

"Glory brings me pictures every day." She sucked on an orange slice. When the juice dribbled down her chin he wiped it away. "Thank you. She loves that child, Jared."

"She loves all of them. I warned her about getting too emotionally involved but it does no good."

"Of course not." Sister blinked. "Loving children is part of who Glory is. She couldn't stop herself even if she wanted to. But Bennie has taken up permanent residence in her heart. She talks about him nonstop, revels in his accomplishments as if she's his mother."

He set his fruit aside, picked up another dish and studied her.

"You're worried."

"So are you." She put down the paper-thin slice of watermelon, picked up a biscuit instead. "What about when the boy's parents come for him?"

He took a bite of his chicken salad. "His parents and sister died in the same fire that injured him. I don't think he has any family."

The biscuit tumbled out of her fingers as she laid her head against the pillows, too weary to sit up unaided. "Whoever it is, she will be hurt. I don't want that, Jared. I don't want to see her suffer anymore."

Anymore? What did that mean?

She'd eaten almost nothing. He lifted her plate away.

"Glory is a doctor. She knows all about separation." He eyed dessert. Cherry pie. An hour of swimming should work it off.

"You like her, don't you, Jared?" Sister's brown eyes probed deeply.

For some reason he hesitated before answering.

"Of course. She's a good doctor."

"I don't mean just as a doctor. I mean as a person." Her frail hand brushed his cheek. Her smile bloomed. "I can tell."

Why deny it?

"Yes, I do like her."

"Tell me why."

"She's like a change of air, a fresh breeze. She's so completely herself, no matter what. She doesn't let anything stop her from getting what she wants." Which bothered him a lot.

"You balance each other so well," Sister murmured. "Your strengths and hers combine, you bring out the best in each other."

He put down his cup, studied that oh-so-blasé look. "No."

"I beg your pardon?" Innocence personified. As if.

"Do not start thinking in those terms, Philomena."

"I'm too old for you to call by my first name."

"Too old and too crafty by far," he agreed. "But I'm serious. GloryAnn is a great doctor, a very nice person and I admire her greatly, but it ends there."

"Does it?" Sister's lids lifted to show him her ingenuousness. "Whoever suggested anything else?"

Jared opened his mouth then clamped it shut around a hard roll, which the woman under discussion had included with his meal.

"Are you still mourning Diana?" Her whisper-soft question filled the room.

In that moment he accepted the truth. "I loved her very much. I miss her. But she's gone now and I can't bring her back. That part of my life is over. I've accepted that."

"And Nicholas?"

The throb of pain still shafted deeply into his soul, but Jared could regroup more quickly now.

"You still blame God for taking him." It was not a question.

"Not only God," he grated, swallowing past the lump in his throat.

"Give up on revenge, Jared. It only hurts you."

She knew as well as he that he could not do that without betraying those he'd loved. So Jared calmly continued with his meal.

"Death is such an odd thing." Her voice faded away as if she'd fallen asleep, but rallied moments later. "One day you're here, the next, *pfft!* Time is so precious."

"I thought you believed in Heaven." ·

"Any sane person believes in Heaven. But that's eternity. I'll have all the time I want there. It's here on earth that's the problem."

"Why?"

She struggled to sit up, gladly accepted his hand of support. But when she was comfortable Sister Phil didn't let go; instead she wrapped her other arm around his neck and drew him close.

"I love you as if you were my own son," she whispered.

"I love you, too, Philomena." A tear dribbled down her cheek and he lifted it away on the tip of his index finger, stunned by the wealth of feeling she was exposing. "What's wrong? Why are you crying? Are you in pain?"

She nodded but stayed his hand when he would have reached for the syringe.

"Not that kind of pain. My heart hurts for you, Jared. Son."

His throat clogged at the love in her sweet voice.

"I see the bitterness, the anger in you, and I know the damage it will do to your heart. You think God is against you, that He wants to punish you, to steal that which you loved. But that is not God's way."

"You don't have to—"

"Hush now," she whispered, finger against his lips. "Let me say what's in my heart."

He nodded.

"No one knows how many days they have on this

earth. Time passes so quickly. Yesterday I was a young girl bound and determined to serve God. Today I am an old woman and I don't know where the time has gone. I did not even do half of what I wanted, accomplished so few of my goals. But time did not wait for me. And it will not wait for you."

"I'll be fine."

"Will you?" Sadness leached the peace from her face, worry etched tiny lines around her eyes. "How, when you refuse to accept the love of the One who loves you most?"

"Phil—"

"True love, the strongest love you will ever know. He is love, everything in Him and around Him and about Him adores you. He cannot be otherwise, for you are His child every bit as much as Nicholas was yours."

"I can't accept that a God of love would have allowed my family to die like that."

"But you must! Don't you see, Jared? It is only in surrender, in accepting that His will is best, however difficult that may be, it is only then that you will truly be free to move on to the future He has prepared for you."

Her strength faded and she withered against the pillows, a mere shadow of the woman he'd known. Jared checked her pulse, opened the drip a little wider to allow more of the sedative to flow. He bathed her forehead with a clean cloth, drew the thin blanket up around her neck.

"Rest now," he whispered, brushing his lips against her cheek.

"Listen to Glory," she murmured, her words slurring as the morphine took effect. "She will help you face the truth. Trust Glory."

Jared kept his vigil until her thin chest rose and

dropped in a rhythm that told him she was resting comfortably. He set the dishes outside her door to be packaged up when the nurse returned, refilled her water jug with ice and tossed out the faded flowers, replacing them with some he cut from her little garden.

Then there was nothing he could do. Nothing anyone could do.

Sister Phil did not have many more days with them. She'd faithfully served God for many years, given herself so that now, at the end, she had nothing left.

Of all people, she did not deserve to suffer this way.

Why? his heart raged. His soul wept at the silence.

At two in the morning, after several emergencies, Glory finally found a free moment to pad down the hallway to the infants' ward to check on Maria. The little girl had been fretful. Glory needed to make sure she was not suffering needlessly.

The night nurse sat sipping a cup of tea.

"Everything okay?" Glory asked as she glanced around the room. Maria's bed was empty. "Where is she?"

The nurse beckoned as she walked across to the half-open patio door that led to an outdoor balcony and pointed. Glory could see someone seated at the far end, in a rocking chair, holding a child. The soft hum of a lullaby carried to them on night-wind zephyrs.

"She was fractious. You were busy, so Dr. Steele came. He's been out there with her for several hours. He seems to have the knack of settling her."

"Apparently."

Since she was no longer needed and was technically off shift, Glory went to sit by Bennie, to watch his little face wrinkle and stretch as dreams flickered through his mind.

"I love you, Bennie," she whispered, brushing his petal-soft cheek with her lips. "And I don't know how to help you."

"Mama?" he moaned.

"Yes, honey. It's Mama," Glory murmured, glad no one was near enough to hear. She rearranged his shirt so it didn't pull against his wound, straightened his blankets. Then there was nothing else to do.

She should go home, go to bed, but she knew she wouldn't sleep. So Glory sat by Bennie's bedside, his hand folded in hers as she prayed for God to help this precious child. But every time her eyes closed she saw Jared Steele folded into a rocking chair far too small for him, cradling a little girl who hurt.

At dawn one of the nurses tapped her shoulder. Glory lifted her head from the bed, rubbed the back of her aching neck. Bennie wiggled when she kissed him, but he didn't wake up. She lifted his red sailboat from the floor, tucked it by his bed. If she hung around longer, she'd wake him. Glory decided to go for a swim.

In her cottage she changed, then tucked her Bible into her beach bag. Sitting on the sand, with the waves lapping at her feet, was the perfect place to talk to God about her confusion. She was almost finished her prayer for Bennie when a rattle on the path behind her drew her from her introspection.

Jared. Judging by the fan of lines around his mouth and the redness of his eyes, he'd also had little sleep.

"Am I disturbing you?"

"Of course not. I'm psyching myself up to go in." She grimaced. "The water always feels cooler in the morning."

"Hmm." Clearly he didn't feel the same for he dropped his towel, waded in and immediately began swimming toward the deep.

"Good morning to you, too," she muttered. But it was too lovely a day to be grumpy, so she swam a few laps, went through her usual aquacize routine and then lazed on her back, watching the fluffy clouds scud across the blue sky.

"Are you still interested in coming to Honolulu today—with me?" Jared asked.

Glory flailed in the water for a moment, surprised that he was so near, that she hadn't heard him approach. His hand grabbed, helped her find her footing.

"Yes, I am. Unless you don't want company."

"It's not that."

But it was something. She could tell from the way his forehead pleated.

"I don't need an escort," she assured him. "Just tell me where and when to meet you and I'll be fine."

"I have a couple of meetings. I'll be tied up most of the day. But we could have dinner later, if you like."

"It's not necessary." What meetings?

"Can you be ready to leave in two hours?"

"Sure."

"Good. See you later." He waded out of the water, toweled down and pulled on a T-shirt and shoes before jogging up the hill.

Suddenly the sea didn't offer the same balm it had before his arrival. Glory emerged from the water chilled, and not just by the air.

Something was wrong and she didn't understand what. Maria? Sister Phil?

God, I feel like I'm missing something. I want to help Jared but I don't want to intrude. Please show me how I can be an extension of You.

She gathered her things, returned home to shower and change, leaving just enough time to check on Bennie. He smiled at her with his usual sunny good humor, handed her the Valentine he'd made with the nurses' help.

"It's lovely, darling." She thanked him with a hug, savoring the feel of his chubby arm around her neck as he laid his cheek against her chest. The other arm he kept tucked at his side, proof that the tightening skin was restricting his range of motion. He clung to her hand as she moved around the ward. Eventually he perched on her knee, waiting for her to read his book.

Bennie's happy gurgle of laughter at the story's silly conclusion squeezed her heart. He was so precious, so dear. How could Jared not help him?

She coaxed him to play finger games until it was almost time to leave.

"Have a wonderful Valentine's party with the nurses, Bennie," Glory whispered in his ear. Bennie was finally persuaded to let go of her hand, but he ran back for a hug just before she walked through the door.

"I think someone has a crush on you." The nurse winked.

"I have a crush on someone, also," Glory told her, heart aching as a nurse encouraged him to toss the ball. He didn't even try to use his injured side.

"I hope you have a bunch of your own kids someday. You're a born mother."

"I think that's a ways off, but I hope so, too." Glory's laugh caught in her throat as she turned, saw Jared's face. His stare bored into her, through her, his eyes glacial chips. "I'm sorry if I made you wait," she apologized.

"You didn't."

They walked to the car without further conversation. He drove silently, perhaps a little too fast, his face like chiseled granite.

Glory held her peace as long as she could but finally blurted out, "Is something wrong?"

"What?" He jerked out of his stupor, twisted his head to look at her, though she couldn't read his expression because of the dark sunglasses. "I'm fine."

"If you say so. Are you going to be tied up with your meetings all day long? I'm only asking," she hurried to explain, "because I wondered if you want to meet for lunch. Of course, I have my cell phone, so if—"

"I'm not sure how it will work out but I anticipate being there all day."

"Oh." Shut down, Glory leaned back in her seat and studied the lush countryside.

After several moments Jared let out a pent-up breath.

"I'm going to a hearing. For Viktor."

Glory caught her breath at his bitter tone.

"He's apparently remorseful, they think maybe even suicidal. The place where he's been serving his time hasn't the medical care he needs, so they want to move him to a lower-security facility."

"Which you don't want."

"No." A sheen of anger radiated from him. "I don't want him to ever leave the walls he's encased in. Especially not now."

"What do you mean 'now'? Has something changed?"

"He claims he's become a Christian."

"You don't believe him?"

"It's a little too convenient. He's been in for three years. Suddenly he's sorry for deliberately ramming their car over a cliff." Jared snorted his derision. "I guess you could say I have a problem with that penitence, yeah."

"Maybe three years has given him the time to realize how wrong he was."

"Maybe." His jaw flexed. "I know what you're going to say, Glory."

"Do you?"

"God forgives us if we ask Him," he singsonged. "He doesn't put stipulations on what He will and won't forgive. Even the most heinous sinner can be forgiven if he asks."

"Can't argue with that."

"Can't or won't? Doesn't matter because even if someone's forgiven or not, he still has to pay for his crime. At least in our society."

"And you want Viktor to serve his full time in maximum security."

"Every last second," he affirmed bitterly.

"When will you be satisfied, Jared?"

Silence.

"In—twenty years?"

"Twenty-five."

"Okay, twenty-five. After twenty-five years have passed, are their deaths more forgivable? Or is that simply the amount of time you need to cool down?"

"Stop it."

"I really want to know." She modulated her voice,

striving to sound interested without condemning. "How long do you need before you'll be satisfied? Or is what you're really after something entirely different?"

"I don't know what you mean."

He knew. Glory could hear it in his voice.

"Stop pretending, Jared. The only thing that will satisfy you is this man's death."

"Yes!" He ripped off his sunglasses, tossed them on the dashboard.

Glory fought back her emotions, prayed for the right words.

"What if you die first? What if you wait years and years and you never get to see him pay the ultimate price?" The thought of Jared wasting his life brought tears. "At the end of your life, when there are no more days, no more hours, when you've wasted every moment you've had—will the cost of your hate be worth it then?"

"It's not like that. I'm not frozen into revenge." He shot her a look of pure frustration. "Is it so wrong to want justice?"

"Everybody wants justice."

"So?"

"There's a difference between wanting to see justice served and putting your life on hold until it happens."

"What's your answer?" he sniped.

"You won't like it."

"When did that ever stop you?" His smile held no mirth.

"Forget about him. Diana and Nicholas died. It was a terrible thing that shouldn't have happened, but it did and there's nothing you can do to change it, nothing you can do to undo the damage or heal the wounds. In a way it's like a burn."

"A burn?"

"I know it sounds a little odd, but think about it. A burned child arrives at Agapé. What do we do?"

"We clean the burn, we assess the damage, we try to treat it."

"Yes. But we can't heal it. The skin has to grow on its own. We try to support that process, of course, but nothing modern medicine has can undo the burn. Only time heals. With God's help."

Jared eased onto the freeway, his focus on the road. He steered around traffic, found a parking space and pulled in.

But Glory couldn't get out. Not yet.

"Diana and Nicholas are in Heaven, Jared. They've never been anyplace better, happier. Their healing is complete."

"Am I supposed to be glad that I can't wish my son happy birthday? That I can't wish my wife happy anniversary?" he snapped.

"Today?" Glory almost groaned as his head jerked once, in the affirmative.

Oh, why hadn't she shut her mouth?

Help me say the right thing.

"Nicholas is having the best birthday he could have with his Heavenly Father, Jared. Do you imagine, even for a second, that you love him or Diana more than God does?"

She opened the car door, stepped out and carefully closed it.

"I'll be free whenever you want to return. Just call my cell."

As soon as he nodded, Glory turned and quickly walked

down the street. She came to a coffee shop. Coffee in hand, she searched a street directory for the nearest church. She needed the precious peace of a sanctuary now.

She was head over heels in love with a man who would never love her the way she yearned to be loved.

Chapter Ten

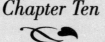

The stuffy room wasn't much bigger than his largest treatment room at Agapé.

Jared shuffled in his chair struggling to concentrate on what the members of the hearing board were saying. But he couldn't get his mind off Glory's last words.

They've never been happier.

They rattled round and round his head until he wanted to scream.

"I understand you have something you wanted to say, Dr. Steele?"

Jared jerked out of his introspection. Everyone watched him. Only by forcing every muscle to respond was he able to rise as he wrestled to pronounce the damning words he'd thought lay on the tip of his tongue ready to pour out.

They weren't there.

"Today is…was my anniversary. It would also have been my son's sixth birthday. Valentine's Day. It's supposed to be a day to share love, but I don't feel that."

Can't undo the damage or heal the wound.

"Dr. Steele? Are you all right?"

Jared wasn't. Inside he was coming apart, fracturing into a million pieces. He didn't want to remember them here, not with *him* watching.

"I'm sorry," he blurted out. "I can't do this. Not today."

He got himself outside as quickly as possible, stumbled down the steps and toward his car. Once there he climbed inside, drew in great gulps of air until his heart rate settled and he could see through the wash of tears that left his face damp.

He opened the glove box to search for a tissue, saw the photo lying on the floor.

Nicholas.

The yearning to hold that wiggling body in his arms, to brush his lips over the dark head, to grasp that chubby little hand in his—his heart sobbed.

Then the world righted itself and he saw the bandage.

Bennie's picture.

Glory must have dropped it.

"Jared?" Her voice sounded so near.

He twisted his head, met her compassionate gaze.

"What are you doing here?"

"My appointment was in there." He jerked his head toward the court building, which suddenly felt miles away. "You?"

"I was in the church." She pointed at a side street but her focus remained fixed on him. "Is something wrong?"

"I'm fine." He composed himself with a few deep breaths, reached across and opened the car door. "I was going to pick up some Valentine treats for the kids. Want to come?"

"Yes!" She climbed in. "Also, I want to get something special for Sister Phil. I know she probably won't be able to eat chocolate. But I want something really nice for her, anyway."

As they fell into their easy banter, the gloom lifted. Jared headed for the Aloha Tower.

"Will you help me choose a gown for her to wear in bed? The one she has is difficult for her."

Glory beamed with excitement. "This will be fun."

"More than you know." He expected her curious glance. "This mall has the best gelato in town."

"I think I like gelato."

"You've never had it?" She shook her head. "Then we'll order some for our dessert."

"Dessert?" She frowned. "Jared, I really want to get back in time for dinner this evening."

"Oh." It was obvious she was up to something. Her green eyes sparked an orange ember in their depths that hinted at mischief and intrigued him. "What's the rush?"

"I hired some people to put on a puppet show. I want to watch it with the children."

"A puppet show?"

"Kahlia told me about them. They're going to rig up an outdoor stage on the side. Those who can't go outside will have their beds wheeled to the windows."

Always the kids.

"Perhaps we could make up a couple of piñatas," he offered, remembering Nicholas's delight the day Diana had insisted on hanging one.

"Really?" She practically danced out of the car and into the shopping center.

When Glory turned left, he took her arm, steered her in the opposite direction, toward the candy store.

"Oh, my." She began assembling her order.

Jared kept the other clerk busy with his own chocolate order for the staff. Diana had started the tradition and he'd kept it up, knowing he didn't thank them often enough. Then he and Glory put their heads together and chose the piñatas and their contents. By the time they were finished it was well past noon and he was starving.

They made a quick detour so Glory could help him choose the perfect gown for Sister Phil. In return he helped her select a bouquet of Sister's favorite flowers.

"Lunch?" he suggested, juggling packages.

Glory sniffed the flowers she held, nodded. "Where?"

"Follow me." He led her to a fast-food chain.

"You're kidding." She stared at him deadpan.

"I know we medical people are always preaching healthy lifestyles and I do try, but I'm craving a burger and fries." He backtracked quickly. "If you'd rather have a salad or something, I think they have it on the menu."

"Don't even think it." An imp of mischief danced in those remarkable eyes.

After lunch Jared led her toward the gelato shop.

"Choose whatever you like."

"Blackberry," Glory ordered after one swift glance at the menu. A young woman hurried away to fill her request. "What are you having?"

Amusement flared in her eyes when their server didn't bother to ask him, simply dished up a giant serving of chocolate hazelnut.

"I see you've been here before," she teased as he held the door open for her.

"Once or twice," Jared admitted. He chose a table with chairs in the sun.

Glory insisted he taste her treat, no doubt so he'd reciprocate. Jared quashed that hope.

"I'd offer you some of mine but I never share anything chocolate."

"Hmm. You're going to need to swim a lot of laps to work that off," she hinted, holding out her dish and blinking in a femme fatale parody. "Let me help you out."

"Back off, woman. I'll buy you your own dish if you want, but you're not getting mine, so stop drooling."

"Some mothers should have taught their sons to share." She scraped the sides of her dish noisily.

"Some doctors from the Arctic shouldn't be so fond of frozen food."

"Some doctors are like the pot calling the kettle black," she shot back. "I'm ready to leave whenever you are prepared to admit you can't possibly finish that entire dish yourself."

He ate it all, just to prove a point.

"Feel free to call on Dr. Xavier's service later, when your stomach aches."

"Not gonna happen." The day was turning out better than expected.

"You didn't tell me how your meeting went," she murmured gently when they were back in the car, heading home.

"I left early." Jared changed the subject to preparation of the piñatas. They decided there should be three sites. "But how can we make it so they'll all have a swing?"

Glory chuckled. "Hang the youngest ones' piñata on an IV pole."

"Brilliant, Doctor. And the others?"

She tilted her head back, closed her eyes. "I'll think of something," she promised.

But she fell asleep instead.

Jared cut his speed so her long hair didn't whip quite so hard in the wind. She slept deeply, thick lashes resting on her sun-kissed cheeks, lips slightly parted. Her small capable hands lay loosely in her lap atop the picture of Bennie.

When he was with Glory he could almost forget.

Almost.

But then something—Bennie's picture, holding Maria and knowing he'd never again be a father—would trigger the anger and he'd be right back where he'd been, fighting the bitterness, the unanswered questions, the helpless feelings that rendered him impotent. Then the rage would drag at his soul, demanding justice.

Forget? How could he forget when there were so many reminders?

And yet, as Jared considered the afternoon and the many times he'd spoken of Diana, of solutions she'd employed, when he'd remembered Nicholas chortling so hard he'd made them all laugh—at those times the pain was bittersweet. Still buried deep inside his heart, but bearable.

For the first time Jared pushed past all the pat answers he'd so easily fed himself and searched for the underlying reason that insisted he ensure Viktor would not escape justice.

The truth—he would never be free.

Because he was responsible for a child's death as much as Viktor was.

Because he needed to prove he wasn't like Viktor.

Because he was.

Jared took the turn to Agapé a little too fast. The jerk of the wheels over the bumpy road woke Glory.

"I'm a lousy companion," she apologized. "I didn't sleep much last night. I guess it caught up with me."

"Next time don't spend the night huddling beside Bennie," he ordered, insides churning. "Shall we visit Sister Phil before we go to the mission?"

"Sure."

They arrived just as the nurses were changing shifts.

"I thought Leilani told me Sister Phil couldn't afford private care," Glory murmured. "Not that it's any of my business, but if someone's taking a collection, I'd like to chip in, too."

That was Glory—give and then give some more.

"Don't worry," he told her, taking her arm to escort her inside. "You weren't left out. It's been taken care of."

"Oh." She gave him an odd uncertain glance then turned away.

Sister Phil looked brighter, though Jared could see signs the cancer was winning.

"We brought you a Valentine's gift, Philomena."

"Two, actually." Glory plopped her bouquet in the vase a nurse handed her and held it so Sister could smell the fragrance.

"Lovely, but I don't need gifts. Seeing you two is enough."

Jared realized she'd noticed his hand on Glory when they'd entered. He almost groaned.

Don't think it, he wanted to tell her. He set the gift bag with the tissue-wrapped gown on her lap instead.

"This is for you, too."

With trembling hands she lifted the gown free of its tissue and touched the silken threads as if afraid they'd disintegrate.

"I've never worn anything so fine." She lifted her head, her smile tremulous. "Thank you, my dears. Thank you so much."

She reached out to Jared with one hand, Glory the other. Sister drew them close, pressed her lips against their cheeks, her eyes glossy with unshed tears.

"You two make an old woman very happy. But you must go to the mission. I hear the children are very excited about a special surprise for tonight."

"You always find out." Jared decided Glory seemed a little teary-eyed, too. "Don't ever try to keep secrets around her. She can ferret out the truth faster than any street-savvy cop."

"I have my sources." Sister Philomena crossed her arms over her chest, winked at them.

Glory's laughter reached the rafters. She hugged the old woman, brushed her lips across her forehead.

"You're a wonder, all right. You remind me of my father sometimes. He had a way of figuring out every secret the congregation tried to keep." A sad little smile flickered across her lips. "I can still hear his laughter sometimes. Big, boisterous. He enjoyed a good laugh."

"I wish I'd known him. And your mother." Sister patted her hand. "She must have been a very selfless woman to have given her life to save you."

Given her life? Jared gulped. He'd had no idea of the tragedy Glory had experienced, even accused her once of not understanding his loss. He'd been so busy drowning in his own sorry world he'd ignored everyone else's. He made a vow to finally look through the personnel file Elizabeth had sent the week before Glory had arrived.

"You're tired and we must go. I'll stop by later," Glory promised. She was almost at the door when Sister Phil's forceful tone stopped her.

"No. Don't stop by tonight, Glory. I don't feel up to a chat. The nurses and I played chess today and it wore me out." She smoothed the blanket with her fingers, not looking at them.

Jared's warning radar zipped to red alert. Sister was up to something.

Glory looked crushed. "I don't want to intrude."

"You could never intrude, my dear. But go celebrate this loving day with the children. Soak in the excitement on those little faces so you can tell me when I see you tomorrow."

"All right." Glory tossed him a questioning glance.

"I'll be there in a moment."

She nodded. "Good night, Sister."

"Good night, my dear. God bless you."

Jared waited, peering through the window until he could see Glory standing by his car, far out of earshot. Then he faced Sister Phil.

"Don't try to match-make, Philomena."

"I would never dare—"

"You would dare that and more besides. But don't do it." Conscious of the nurse standing just outside the door, he hesitated to say more, though the warning had to be given.

Sister Phil watched him with hawk's eyes. "She's a lovely girl, a wonderful doctor. You suit each other."

"No."

"Do you ever get lonely, Jared? Don't you want to have your own family, care for someone and have them care for you?"

"I had that," he reminded her.

"I'm not talking about the past," she reprimanded sharply. "I'm speaking of the future. You didn't die with Diana and Nicholas."

"I should have."

"Don't be ridiculous," she snapped. "And don't try to play God."

She was furious. That shocked him. He'd never seen Sister Philomena really angry in all the years he'd known her.

"You can't bury yourself in the past, Jared, no matter how hard you try."

"I'm not burying myself."

She studied him for several moments then crossed her arms over her chest.

"I suppose you went to the hearing." She waited for his nod, made a face. "Of course. You had to dig the hole a little deeper, eh?"

"I walked out."

She brightened. "Well, that's progress."

"Not because of any altruistic reason. I simply couldn't sit there and look at him without wanting to wring his neck. I was so angry, I couldn't even remember what I was going to say, so I bolted."

"Good. Better such words remain unspoken."

"It's not over," he warned her quietly.

"Jared, please don't harden your heart. Let it go."

He closed his fingers around hers, pressed gently.

"I'm aware that you think it's wrong to want him to suffer, to pay for what he did. But that's the way I feel." He inhaled, swallowed and confessed. "Maybe because I'm as much to blame as him."

"You aren't to blame!"

"I killed his son." Jared wouldn't let her interrupt. "I didn't mean to but it was my hand that made those incisions, my decision that he was fit to handle the operation. His death is on my conscience and there's no denying that."

"I'm going to say something I should have said long ago." Sister drew herself erect in the bed. "You're trying to escape, to find a way to explain God's will. It won't work. Jesus prayed 'Not my will, but Yours'. You have to pray the same thing. You can't change it, you can't make it more palpable. All you can do is accept that God wanted it this way."

With great difficulty Jared kept his lips clamped together.

"Until you surrender your will, your right to know, your right to get justice—until you hand that all to God and tell Him that whatever He decides will be fine by you, until then you will not find peace."

There was nothing he could say so Jared wished her good-night and left, aware of the tears that tumbled down her cheeks when he turned his back.

"Is she all right?" Glory's troubled gaze rested on the cottage.

"Yes." He drove them to Agapé, carried in their piñatas and helped Glory stuff them.

They organized the children into groups and moved from ward to ward to allow each child to have a turn. The kids laughed and sang, teased each other and shared the candies and toys. Kahlia and Pono were in the thick of it, lending a helping hand here, a lap there, blissful grandparents to anyone who needed them.

Glory moved from one child to the next with a special touch, a word, a reminder. But it was Bennie she always returned to, it was him she spent the longest time with. And Jared knew she loved the boy every bit as much as any mother does her child.

A cold skitter of quiet snaked up Jared's spine as Bennie flailed with the bat, trying to hit the piñata with one hand only because he couldn't raise the other high enough. In that moment Glory looked at him with such pleading he had to look away to stop from making a promise he wouldn't, couldn't keep.

After a boisterous meal, the children learned puppeteers were coming. Wide-eyed, eager, they assembled on the patio. Those who couldn't walk waited on the open balconies above. Glory dashed about for a blanket for this one, an extra pillow for that, determined each patient would not miss a moment. When she finally sank down on the ground, Bennie sat beside her.

Jared had no idea what the program was about. He only knew he had to get away, do something to quiet the inner trauma that taunted him. He tried studying her file but it only made him recall the shattered look on her face. Finally he closed up his office, left.

Since Potter was on call, Jared changed into his trunks and jogged down to the beach. The full moon lit the cove in a silvery glow. He swam until his lungs burned like fire and his body wilted with exhaustion. Finally he crawled out, wrapped his towel around his shoulders and huddled on a rock about four feet above the water.

A kaleidoscope of Glory-pictures flickered through his mind. He'd come here hoping to get his mind off Glory but it wasn't working. Instead he saw her doubled up with laughter, teasing, in a fit of the giggles, empathizing, caring and silently weeping.

He couldn't care about her. She was carefree, happy. She didn't need someone like him weighing down her life. She would be gone in a few months, back to the Arctic.

She deserved children in her life, lots of them. She deserved a man who could give her her heart's desire.

And that man would never be him.

Maybe it would be better if he left Agapé.

Left. Jared studied stars flickering in the dark velvet sky as the idea mushroomed. He wouldn't go right away, of course. He'd wait to make sure Viktor stayed behind bars, until Glory left. He'd tell Elizabeth he'd stay as long as it took to find a replacement. Then he'd leave the islands, find a place to practice medicine that was arm's length, where the patients didn't grab your heart and squeeze it every single day.

He'd do his job the best he could but he'd never expose himself to the pain he'd felt here.

A noise from below drew Jared's attention. Glory stood at the edge of the water, testing its warmth with one toe. After a moment she tossed her towel aside and ran into the water's embrace, laughing as the waves wrapped round her.

She paddled across the cove, twisting and turning in a private game that sent her diving beneath the surface then bursting back up like a sea nymph in search of treasure, golden hair streaming down her back.

Jared watched unabashed, an unseen spectator to her joy in the water, the moonlight, the ebb and flow of the world around them. After a while he couldn't resist the opportunity to share this moment with her.

Soundlessly he stepped down off the rock and slid into the water, moving through it without splashing until he was behind her. Then he waited for her to spot him so she wouldn't be frightened.

"Hello." That all-inclusive smile beamed in a shaft of moonlight.

"Do you mind if I join you?"

"Not at all. This is too lovely to enjoy alone." She stretched out on her back, pointed. "Do you know what that constellation is? I don't recognize it."

"The Southern Cross."

"My father loved stargazing but he never showed me that one. It's exquisite."

She was far lovelier than any combination of stars, but Jared didn't say that. Instead he swam along beside her, content to share her happiness.

"Thank you for finding the paddling pool. The kids enjoy splashing around in it."

"No problem."

"Really? How did you manage to get it in your car?"

"It was Nicholas's pool, though he never used it much."

"Oh. I'm—"

"He loved water. Took after me in that, I guess. Diana grew up here, so to her it was no big deal to have an ocean nearby. But I used to swim twice every day. Nicholas would beg to come in and sitting him in that paddling pool didn't work."

The words poured out, startling him. She was so easy to talk to.

"Aggressive like his daddy, hmm?" she teased.

"Spoiled rotten," he agreed with a smile. "What we didn't give in to, his grandparents did. We couldn't seem to deny him anything."

"Why should you?" Her hand brushed his chest as she turned on her side. "I've just realized I don't know much about you. Where did you grow up?"

"Great Falls, Montana. My mother was a secretary to a lawyer." He kept pace with her strokes. "She was big on education, wanted me to go to college, but I don't think even she imagined I'd go to school for so long."

"And your father?"

"Never knew him and she didn't talk about him."

"You didn't ask?" Glory sounded puzzled.

"I tried a couple of times, but when I saw how sad it made her I decided I didn't need to know. She died keeping her secret."

"I'm sorry."

"Thank you." She'd spoken of her father, so he decided to probe. "What was your father like?"

"A cross between a lovable teddy bear and a taskmaster," she told him quietly. "He didn't like shirkers but he believed in enjoying life. He died after my first year in medical school."

"Now I'm sorry. I didn't mean to bring back sad memories."

"Mostly they're not." She flapped her arms, rotating

her prone body in a circle. "I thought at first that I'd die, too. I was alone, in debt, with no way to finish my training. That's when Elizabeth showed up, offered to pay for it all. In exchange, I agreed to give her back six months. That's why I'm here."

"And when you're finished you'll go back up north." Why did those words hurt?

"Yes. I have to."

"Have to?"

"I promised my mother."

Unsure of what to say next but not yet ready to leave, Jared floated beside her and tried to imagine Glory as the only child of missionaries. It took a while to notice she'd headed to shore.

He caught up in a few crawl strokes. "Going in?"

"I'm chilly. I brought a thermos of tea. You're welcome to share if you want."

"Thanks." He retrieved his towel from his perch, laid it beside hers then sank down. Glory leaned away from him, squeezed out her hair, looped it to the top of her head and held it there with some kind of clip. Then she tugged on the terry dress she'd worn from her cottage, sat down beside him and reached for her bag.

"Much better." Her chattering teeth gave lie to the words.

After twisting the top off a thermos, she filled the lid with steaming liquid. He caught the hint of mint when she passed it to him.

"You first."

Jared had never particularly cared for tea, but now, sitting next to her, it seemed like ambrosia.

"Thank you." He sipped twice then handed back

the cup, knowing she needed the warmth to chase away her chills.

Glory cradled the cup in her hands, the steam caressing her face as she gazed out over the water.

"Sitting here like this, with the palms fluttering and the smell of plumeria on the wind, you'd never believe that somewhere in the world bombs are going off and children are starving, would you?"

"I guess we forget about that pretty easily."

"May I ask you something?"

He studied her profile, the way her nose tilted just the slightest bit at the end, the angle of her chin jutting out to take whatever life handed her.

"I guess."

"Do you ever wish you could hide out for a while?"

The hushed words surprised him. Was she unhappy here?

Immediately Jared chastised himself. He'd always assumed she was content, never once imagined she hid a secret desire to get away.

"Glory, I'm sure Elizabeth wouldn't force you to stay." A fist punched him in the gut. If she went—

When, Jared reminded himself. When she went.

"I don't want to leave!" She turned on him so fast the tea spattered her legs. Fortunately it had cooled somewhat and she could simply brush it away. "That isn't what I meant at all."

Relief washed through him. He struggled to remain impassive, thankful when she turned away to replace the lid on the thermos.

"I meant—" she nibbled on her bottom lip "—every so often don't you wish you could stop the world and savor things? Like tonight. The sky, the moonlight, the peace. Even the dolphins." She pointed out to sea.

The black forms surged and plunged then disappeared.

"Tonight's a perfect diamond, soon lost in a string of fantastic jewels. You need time to appreciate it, to sit back and enjoy the preciousness of this moment before it gets buried among a whole lot of others. I'm so lucky to be here." She hugged her arms around her drawn-up knees and sighed as if she'd been handed a crown.

Then she looked at him.

"Thank you for sharing this with me."

Her green eyes drew him like a magnet, pulling him forward until his lips met hers.

Jared's fingers angled her cheek so he could trail his lips over her feather-soft skin, breathe in her mint-scented breath then return for another taste of her lips.

Glory inched away, just enough to search his face for one infinitesimal moment before her hands lifted to loop around his neck and she returned his kiss, calling to the needy part of him he kept tucked away, protected.

Kissing her was like trying to hold a butterfly. Once moment she was there and he could almost put his arms around her, the next she was gone. She drew away and cupped his jaw in her palm, fingers grazing across his beard-roughened skin as she searched his face for answers.

"Why did you do that?"

Good question. He decided on honesty.

"Because you're beautiful and I wanted to."

After a long time had passed she nodded. Her hand dropped to her lap and she turned back to stare at the ocean. Once she shivered and he slung his arm around her shoulders, hugging her against his side, offering his warmth.

Glory remained beside him, silent until a shooting star arced across the sky and tumbled into the ocean. Then with a heavy sigh she straightened.

"Back to reality."

Jared rose, offered his hand to help her up. She took it, held on even when she stood facing him.

"I wish you a wonderful future, Jared." She curled her fingers around his, squeezed. "I wish you happiness and joy. But most of all I wish you peace."

Then she gathered up her things and started walking up the hill toward her cottage. After a moment Jared caught up, matching her stride until they reached her front door.

"Good night," she whispered. She tottered on tiptoe, brushed her lips against his then turned and walked inside. The door swished closed behind her.

And he was alone in the night.

Jared walked to his own place deep in thought. He sat out in his garden for ages, struggling to fathom what she'd meant by those words.

They'd sounded like farewell.

But Glory had almost four more months before she left Agapé.

So why did it seem as if she'd just left him?

Chapter Eleven

"She doesn't have long, does she?"

Elizabeth Wisdom stood outside Sister Phil's cottage, her face streaked with tears.

"No."

"Will she last until Easter?"

This was only the middle of March. Easter was weeks away.

Glory chose not to answer. Instead she folded one of the blue-veined hands into her own.

"You have to enjoy the time you have now," she murmured. "She's very weak but she insists on talking, so if you can just listen."

"She'll know I'm pandering to her." Elizabeth's weary smile flashed, followed by a sniff. "We always used to argue. Phil usually won. She looks so much worse than she did the last time I was here. I never expected it to happen so fast."

"You've been here all night, you're tired." She waved to Kahlia, knowing the older woman had already made arrangements for Elizabeth to stay with them. "Go and rest now. I'll stay with Sister Phil for a while."

"You'll call if—"

"Yes. Go on now." She smiled as Kahlia enfolded Elizabeth in her loving arms and guided her to the waiting car. Inhaling a deep breath, she entered the small cottage, went directly to Sister's bedside. "Hello."

"Ah, Glory. I'm so glad to see you." She reached up, touched Glory's cheek. "You're getting so thin, child. Whatever is wrong? Are you not well?"

"I'm fine." She tried to make a joke of it. "I sunbathe and swim and eat fantastic food. Why wouldn't I be well?"

"I can think of one reason. It's Jared, isn't it? He's gone to Honolulu again, hasn't he?"

Glory didn't answer.

"I'd hoped he'd given up on his push for revenge." She drooped back against her pillows, her face drawn, sad. "Ah, well, what's the use of asking why."

"I think it's my fault," Glory admitted.

"Yours?" Sister Phil's frown deepened. "Tell me why you think this, my dear."

"It's Bennie." Glory gulped. "He's contracted an infection in the muscle. I—I blamed Jared for causing it."

"Oh, dear."

"I know it isn't his fault, but if only he'd do the surgery—I've been studying the videos, I know it's feasible." She stared at the floor. "But it won't be for much longer. Bennie's forming keloids that are restricting muscle movement."

"You could remove them?"

"Yes, but they'll simply grow back. Jared's procedure is the only method of grafting I know of that will return the use of his arm and contain the regrowth. But Bennie can't wait forever, Sister."

"You love him very much, don't you?" Sister Phil's stern face softened.

"I love Bennie so much. If I could, I'd do the operation myself, but—"

"Dear Glory, I was referring to Jared."

"Jared?" She pretended confusion.

"You love him. I see it in your eyes. I hear it in your voice. That's why his quest for justice hurts you so much."

Glory sank onto a nearby chair, too weary and heartsick to pretend anymore.

"You should see him with little Maria, Sister. He becomes a different man. He's gentle, tender. Nobody could protect her welfare better."

"Is that why you've pulled away from him?"

"I see who he could be," Glory admitted. "But I hate who he'll become if he continues like this."

"He cares for you, too, my dear."

Glory didn't want to upset Sister, so she pretended she hadn't heard.

"Why must he keep pushing, letting the hate take over?"

"He's trying to shape his world." Sister reached out for her water glass.

Glory helped her sit up to drink. Then she eased the frail woman back onto the bed.

"Jared feels responsible for their deaths. Going after Viktor is his way of making sure no one else pays for his error."

"But he didn't make an error. At least I didn't see one.

And apparently neither did the medical review board because they exonerated him."

"People can tell you the truth over and over, but if you're convinced otherwise in your heart, you'll never accept it. That's where Jared is now. Only God can change his heart." She smiled. "Are you still enjoying your stay here, Glory?"

"I love it here. It's as if I've come home."

"Perhaps you have."

"Why do you think God brought me here, Sister?"

"Tell me what you think."

"When Elizabeth first asked me I thought it was because He was giving me the opportunity to learn Jared's procedure. You can't imagine what a boon it would be to the patients up north."

"You doubt that now?"

"Jared hasn't done the procedure even once since I've been here. Basically I'm a sometimes pediatrician, often acting as a kind of recreational therapist." She shook her head. "Don't misunderstand, I love the work. I just thought it would be—more."

"Why do you think God led you here?"

"I don't know. Everything seems mixed up."

"Because you love Jared."

"But I can't!" Glory tugged her hair free of its band and rubbed the aching spot. "When my six months are up I *will* go home, Sister. Now more than ever it's urgent that I return."

"Why now?"

"There is no doctor servicing Tiska," she explained. "I had a letter last week. The visiting doctor quit, the regional doctor is ill. There is no medical treatment for my friends. They've pinned their hopes on me and I can't disappoint them. I won't."

"And besides, you promised your mother." Sister Phil sighed. "It is a difficult situation."

Glory struggled to repress the surge of love she battled daily.

"I do care for Jared. But a relationship between us would never work."

"Why?"

"Because he's still in love with his wife. Because he'll stay here and I'll leave in three months. It's impossible."

"God specializes in the impossible, Glory. But something else plagues you."

"What if I go back and I don't enjoy it? What if I end up hating being there? Maybe I've been spoiled by all this sun and sea."

Sister Phil's croak of laughter brought the nurse running.

"I'm fine," she reassured the stressed woman. "Focus on God, Glory." She coughed into her lace-fringed handkerchief then fixed Glory with a stern look. "Now, what other lies has the Tempter been throwing at you?"

She was the doctor, the healer. She'd come to help Sister Phil, not to dump all her woes on a delicate sickly old woman. But Glory couldn't stop.

"What if Bennie dies?" she whispered. "I think my heart would rip apart if that happened. How can I blame Jared for being so consumed with revenge when I don't know that I wouldn't be exactly the same?"

"You're afraid to love?"

"I already love both of them. I'm afraid that letting them into my heart is going to cost me too much. I want to obey God. But I also want love, a family, a husband. Is that wrong?"

"Glory, God made you with a special place in your heart for love to fit. Of course it isn't wrong."

"Then why am I so conflicted?"

"Perhaps because you have to wait to understand what He would have you do. Just as Jared can't comprehend why God would take Diana and Nicholas, you can't see into the future and figure out what He has planned."

"What do I do?"

"Talk to Him. You are His precious daughter. He will show you the way."

Remorse gripped her as the parchment eyelids fluttered.

"I've kept you too long," she whispered. "Rest now."

"I'll have plenty of time to rest soon." But Sister closed her eyes anyway.

Glory pressed her lips against the alabaster forehead, then left, going back to the mission. At least there she could keep busy.

By the time the last case was safely dealt with Glory could barely stand.

"You and Dr. Xavier go rest," she told Dr. Potter. "I'll cover for a while. If I need you, I'll page."

"I intend to speak to Elizabeth about this, Glory." Fredrick Potter was furious. "This is the third time this week we've had to cover for Jared. He's the head man, he should be here, not off in Honolulu."

"Please," she begged. "Let me handle it."

"We're all tired, overworked. We need the other two doctors here. You're covering twice your load and then some. If you get sick—" He shrugged. "Just talk to him. Soon."

Though she ached to lie down, close her eyes and forget everything, Glory had to see Bennie. She knelt beside his bed, brushed his cheek.

"Good night, sweet boy," she whispered.

"I didn't say my prayers yet, Glory Mom. I thought you weren't coming."

"Of course I was coming. I just had to help some other kids." She brushed her lips against the glossy walnut-toned head. "Is that my new name?"

"Uh-huh. 'Cause my other mom's gone."

Glory lost her voice, struggled with tears.

"Don't you like your name, Glory Mom?"

"I love it, darling. You say your prayers now, while I'm listening."

He folded his hands together as she'd shown him and began talking, his English still somewhat formal, even after the weeks he'd spent here.

"And God bless my Glory Mom. Amen." He blinked his incredibly long lashes, waiting for her approval.

"That was a lovely prayer," she told him. "Thank you."

"Where is Dr. Jared?"

"Um, he's busy, honey."

"I didn't see him the whole day. Is he mad at me?"

"Of course not, why do you ask that?" She pushed back the hair, unable to stop the love that spilled from her heart.

"He gets a mad face when he comes and looks at my shoulder. Today he yelled at the nurse and she didn't do anything. He called me Nicholas. My name's not Nicholas. My name is Bennie."

"Of course that's your name, darling. We all know

that. Dr. Jared is worried about helping all the children, that's all. Sometimes he gets the names mixed up."

"But, Glory Mom, there is no Nicholas here. I asked the nice lady that reads the story. She said Nicholas is gone away."

Oh, poor Kahlia. Glory's heart clenched. She whispered a prayer for the grandmother.

"Yes, he is. But he's very happy. You go to sleep now, sweetie. Tomorrow we've got so many things to do. Puzzles and games and maybe even a walk to see Pono's flowers. Do you know I saw a hummingbird today?"

"I want to see one so I can draw it in my book." Excitement dimmed to pain. "My fingers hurt a lot but I try to keep using them because you asked me to."

"That's very good, darling." She buried her face in his hair until she could regain control. "You must go to sleep now, Bennie."

"Okay." He snuggled down into his pillow, squeezed his eyes shut—for about three seconds. Then his hand touched her face. "Glory Mom?"

"What is it, sweetie?"

"Is God ever going to make me better? I pray and pray but it doesn't work."

"God hears you, Bennie. But we have to be patient until He answers us." Which was exactly what Sister Phil had told her.

"'Cause He's got lots of other people to listen to, right?"

"That's right. Go to sleep now. I love you, Bennie."

"I love you, too." He gave her one last tight hug then settled down. A few moments later his soft snores signaled he was asleep.

Glory moved through each ward, checking every

bed to ensure not one of the precious children felt alone or abandoned. She ended, as she always did, in the infants ward. Maria was fussing as usual so she picked her up, moved to the rocking chair on the balcony and began to hum, something they'd learned settled the little girl immediately.

Glory wasn't sure how long she'd been out there dreaming of one day rocking her own child, when strong arms lifted the precious girl from her arms.

"It's time for you to go to bed, Glory." Jared's low voice murmured in her ear. "Come on, I'll walk you there."

"You're back." She yawned, rose. When his arm circled her waist, she didn't try to regain her independence but leaned on him. "What time is it?"

"Late. Are you all right?" His hand rested against her cheek, cool and comforting.

"I'm fine." She walked beside him down the stairs and out the door, shivering as the sea breeze grazed across her skin. "It's cool tonight."

"Not really." He slung his jacket around her shoulders. "Glory, you feel awfully warm. Are you certain you're all right?"

"Tired," she mumbled, huddling into the warmth his body had left behind. She licked her dry lips. "And thirsty."

"Get ready for bed. I'll make you a hot drink."

Surprised they'd reached her cottage so quickly, she didn't bother to argue but went into her bedroom and changed into a nightgown. A ratty old bathrobe she'd brought from home and never used since arriving in Hawaii offered the perfect insulation. She wrapped it around herself and climbed into bed as Jared knocked on the door.

"Come in." Her voice sounded like a frog's. "Your jacket's on the chair. Thanks." She leaned back on the pillows with a sigh.

Jared carried a thermometer and made her take her temperature.

"I thought so. You've got a fever. Here, take these." He held out two tablets.

Glory washed them down with the water he'd brought. In fact, she drank the whole glass. But now she felt colder.

"Thank you," she whispered, trying to hide her rasping voice. "I'm going to sleep now. If you need me, call me."

"We won't need you, Glory. You rest now."

"Okay." She peeked at him when he tucked the covers around her chin. "Did you get what you wanted today?"

He shook his head.

"Sorry." She yawned, turned her cheek against the pillow and let tiredness swamp her.

Jared didn't say anything. Maybe he was mad at her. Oh, well, she'd have to deal with it tomorrow.

Jared couldn't stop staring at her.

Glory's face bore a fine sheen of sweat, her cheeks two round dots of color. One hand was tucked beneath her ear and he wondered if it ached.

She'd picked up shift after shift, covered for him with any number of excuses. And she'd done it without complaint.

Eight cases, two critical. He should have been here.

Instead, he'd cooled his heels trying to meet with someone from the parole board, hoping to forestall their plan. They'd finally promised to hear him, but when?

As he sat in the small chair and waited for the tablets to take effect, Jared wished he could do as Glory begged and stop this insanity. But he felt as if he were on some kind of crazy roller coaster, attending meeting after fruitless meeting. On nights like tonight, while driving home in the dark, he'd almost convince himself to give up, to forget.

And then he'd remember something, the funeral, that moment when their bodies sank into the ground—anything could trigger the intense rage that fueled his desire for revenge.

He hated it in himself. It was like a disease, a cancer that refused to be cut out. In fact, it grew more intense every time the man's name was mentioned. Even now acid poured into his stomach, feeding the fury.

Jared rose, walked to the bed and laid the back of his hand against Glory's smooth cheek. Hot.

"I got your call." Elizabeth stood in the doorway. "Is she all right?"

"She's got a fever. I gave her something but it's not working yet. We took in some criticals tonight. I should check on them. Can you stay with her?"

"Yes. I'll use the other bedroom if I need to catch some sleep, though I slept half the evening away. Phil doesn't look good, Jared."

"I know." He gathered her into his arms and let her weep on his shoulder until the tears were spent. After the storm, grief lingered in her dark gaze. "She hasn't got much time left. Can you stay?"

Elizabeth nodded, drew back, accepted a tissue and wiped her nose. "I'm a wimp."

"It's a hard time for everybody. Philomena's been our

rock for so long. The mission was her idea. I guess we thought she'd outlast it."

Elizabeth's eyes scoured his face for answers. Finally she drew him out of the room, left the door open a crack.

"It's hard for all of us to think of this place without her."

"And without you." She pulled a piece of paper from her pocket, held it toward him. "What are you doing, Jared?"

"Resigning. I won't leave yet. I'd like to wait until—" He searched for the right way to phrase it. "Until the other matter is settled. But after that, well, I want to go after that, Elizabeth."

"You're sure?"

"Yes." He saw the truth in her eyes. "We both know that without the procedure, I'm not the best man for this job. It's time someone else took over. Someone with bigger ideas, fresh blood."

Someone without an ax to grind.

"So you'll walk away without a second thought."

"No!" He couldn't stand for her to think that her friendship, this place, her cousin, hadn't meant a lot to him. "I'll walk away with a lot of memories, some regrets and the hope that whoever succeeds me will do a much better job."

"I was wrong," she murmured, her chin thrust out. "You're the wimp."

The scorn bit deep but he held her regard, nodded.

"You won't even fight for her?" she asked, head inclined toward the door that led into Glory's room.

"I don't know what you mean."

"Don't lie to me, Jared. You care about her."

He gave it up.

"Yes, I do. But that is irrelevant. She'll return to the Arctic and I'll leave here, find somewhere else."

"And do what? Spend your life hating, mourning, grieving?"

Each word was a barb that sank deep into his skin, made all the worse because Elizabeth was not a harsh woman.

"I won't leave until I see justice served."

She studied him for a moment, shook her head, her eyes sad.

"How arrogant you are. You think that you're the only one who ever got a raw deal? That no one else has the right to want answers, to hold God accountable?" Her harsh truth shocked him. "You ought to talk to the woman in there about hard knocks."

"What do you mean?"

"Did you ever read the file I sent?"

He felt stupid. "I never got around to it."

"You should have. GloryAnn Cranbrook is a study in taking it on the chin and not crumbling. Her mother rescued Glory from a burning building, received third-degree burns to eighty percent of her body. Because of a storm, no medical help could reach her. She died, making Glory promise to return to the North and treat the Inuit."

"She mentioned a promise."

"Really? Did she also tell you that she had just finished her first year when her father was killed?"

He nodded.

"Do you know how he died?" She waited for his response. "He was guiding tourists to see the polar bears so he could scrape together enough money to use for her tuition for another year at medical school. Glory got nothing when he died because he'd already cashed in his life insurance to help pay for her first year. In fact, she was in debt. She would have missed out on her medical career altogether—a woman like that, dedicated, loving, gentle. I wish God had made ten of her."

"She is exceptional."

"Don't offer me platitudes, Jared Steele." Elizabeth glared at him. "I want you to explain to me what gives you the corner on suffering? What gives you the right to stop doing the work God sent you here to do just because you think a man didn't get the punishment he should? Because God in His almighty wisdom didn't explain Himself to you?"

She was furious and he understood. That was the worst of it. Jared could stand back and see how his hate was affecting everyone, but he couldn't stop himself.

"I don't have the answers, Elizabeth. I only know it's what I have to do. What I can't accept is that he is still alive, almost free, that Viktor could walk away with never having paid for taking their lives."

"You can't be that naive." Exasperation clouded her voice.

"Naive?"

"Viktor hasn't walked away, Jared. He has to live with the memories of what he did, of the child he lost. Grief drove him to what he did. Doesn't that spark the least bit of humanity in your soul?"

"I wonder if you'd be so ready to make excuses for me if in my grief I had killed him."

She shook her head, studying him in a silence that stretched out far too long.

"I'm almost glad you won't let yourself care for Glory. She's a fine, strong, courageous woman who tackles life with faith and hope. She needs a man who can walk that path with her, not someone who's always looking back."

"I know," he whispered, wishing with everything in him that he could be that man.

Elizabeth picked her purse off a nearby table.

"I'll make some tea, sit with her for a while."

"Thank you." He turned to leave.

"And Jared?"

Something in her voice made him turn and examine the finely drawn features. He saw the pain crouched there, the knowledge that she, too, would soon be among the grieving.

He also saw love.

"You've always been the son I never had," she whispered. "That will never change. No matter where you go."

"I love you, too," he told her, wishing he could heal the hurt he'd caused her.

Then he left.

The sounds in the other room died away.

Glory lifted her head, heard the soft hum of a woman's voice.

She laid her head back against the pillow and let the words sink in.

"Resigning...I want to go after that, Elizabeth."

Jared was leaving and he hadn't even told her. That kiss, the embrace—none of it meant a thing to him. He didn't care about her, the hospital, the children or even Elizabeth.

Tears rolled down her face.

"Oh, God, please let me go home."

Chapter Twelve

"You've been sick for a week. You can't just jump up from your bed and go back to work," Jared snapped.

"Why not? That's what I'm here for. Besides, I know you have to go to Honolulu today." Glory pointed to the pink message chit that lay on his desktop. "So go. I'll cover you. I'm used to that."

"What does that mean?"

Glory walked over to the door, pushed it closed and leaned her back against it.

"You know exactly what I mean, Jared."

His eyes froze, his mouth pinched.

She ignored the ache in her heart, pushed ahead because it had to be said. "Do you know that Elizabeth is worried the board won't approve the new machine you asked for?"

"Oh?"

"She won't tell you. She doesn't want to burden you. Anyway, what do you care? You're leaving, right?"

"Not yet."

She shrugged as if it didn't matter when he took off.

But every cell in her brain hurried to memorize each detail of his face, the way he walked, the shape of his head.

"She knows it's coming and she's doing her best to accommodate you. It's pretty difficult to recruit when you can't give candidates a firm date, but hey, as long as you're not inconvenienced."

"I didn't expect you to understand."

"Good. Because I don't." She marched across the room, stood in front of him. "Look around, Jared. There are a whole lot of kids here who need attention. But they're not getting what they need because the rest of us are stretched too thin. And we don't have your expertise."

"You're talking about Bennie," he snapped, his eyes narrowing.

"Bennie and Maria and all the rest. When was the last time you actually noticed the kid and not the injury?"

"I see them every day."

She shook her head.

"You see the wounds. You don't see past them to the frightened little soul inside who just wants life to be like it was." She paused for a moment. "You're even ignoring Sister Philomena."

"I was there this morning."

"Were you?" Glory pinned him with the truth. "You dashed in, checked her chart and left when she was barely awake. You couldn't spare the time to sit beside her and just talk."

"I'm busy. I'll see her later."

"And, of course, she'll be waiting. Just as we all will. Sitting waiting for that moment when you have enough time to spare us a second. It really is all about you, isn't it, Jared? Your life, your problems, your needs."

Glory turned away to hide her tears.

"Why are you acting like this?" he demanded, coming up beside her. His hand pressed against her shoulder. "What's wrong?"

She shrugged it off, unable to bear his touch.

"What's wrong? You can't see that everyone has problems. Dr. Xavier received sad news about his daughter. Fredrick needs some time off to relax or he's going to do damage to that bad hip of his. The board is suggesting to Elizabeth that Agapé might be better off closed if we're not doing your procedure. Sister Phil's spirits are low. Bennie is sicker than he's ever been."

Why couldn't he see?

"You are not the only one with problems, Jared."

"I'm sorry," he murmured.

"No, you're not. If you were sorry you'd accept that God deals out justice in His own time and you'd get on with doing what you do best, which, in case you've forgotten, is skin grafting."

"I'm trying—"

"No, you're not trying at all. You're wallowing. But you go ahead, immerse yourself in hate. And after Sister Phil's gone, when it's too late to spend an hour letting her talk, when Bennie's passed the point of viable operating, when Agapé's closed—will you be satisfied then? Will it be enough?"

"You really dislike me, don't you? I thought—" He squeezed his hands closed, shook his head once. "Never mind. I wanted to talk to you about Bennie. I think it might be best if we moved him."

"Move him? Where?"

"Boston, perhaps?"

"What does Boston have that we don't? A new treatment, a way to heal his shoulder?" He shuffled his feet on the floor. Her heart dropped. "The object isn't to get Bennie better treatment, it's to get him out of here, so you won't feel guilty anymore."

"Your opinion of me isn't very high. I'm sorry about that."

It was time to risk all or nothing.

"You're a fantastic doctor, Jared. You have the skills to impact a lot of kids, to bring hope. You could do so much here."

He wasn't responding, so she tried one last time.

"You're a fine man and I care about you a lot. I want you to be happy, to get rid of the shadows and move into the light. I pray that God will lead you back to enjoying your work, to living up to your potential."

"You care—about me?" he asked, his voice quieter than she'd ever heard it.

"Yes, I do." She felt raw, exposed. "We all care, Jared. But we can't help you anymore. Only you can pull yourself out of this miasma of revenge and take back your life."

She walked to the door, dragged it open and stood beside it.

"I hope you don't wait too long," she whispered. "Take it from me that the people who love you are all that really matters."

Caller ID showed a familiar Honolulu number.

"If you're calling about the meeting today, I have to give it a miss."

"It's been rescheduled. I'm calling about something else."

"Oh. What?" Halfway through his signature, Jared paused.

"Viktor wants to see you."

"What?" Face-to-face with the murderer? "Why?"

"He won't say anything other than he needs to speak with you privately."

"No way. I'm not listening to a last-minute plea to let him walk."

"I get the feeling that's not why."

"It doesn't matter why. I won't do it. Now, when's the next date?" He scribbled it down, ended the conversation, grabbed his lunch sack and headed for the beach to think.

The people who love you.

Glory loved him. Was that what she'd meant?

He already knew he loved her, had known for weeks now.

For a moment he let himself imagine the possibilities. Agapé would be a place of laughter and joy because that's who she was. Life would be full and rich and the kids would cluster around her like bees to honey.

The kids.

In that fraction of a second the dream fizzled and died, leaving him alone, empty.

Glory wanted, deserved kids. Lots of them. She would make a wonderful mother.

But he'd lost his chance.

Restless, unable to relax, Jared strode over the uneven ground to Sister Phil's. Glory was right about that, he had been avoiding her.

"Ah, I hoped you'd come." The fingers could barely lift from the bed.

Jared covered them with his own and wondered why he'd stayed away.

"How are you, Phil?"

"Tired." She licked her parched lips. "I want to go home."

"You are home," he whispered, sad to see her so disoriented.

Sister Phil's smile flashed as bright as it ever had.

"This is not my home, Jared," she wheezed. "Not my real home. I want to go to be with my Lord. Then I shall truly be home."

"I'll miss you."

"Dear boy. My body will be gone but I'll be here still. In the memories, in the flowers we planted. In the love we shared. In your heart."

"Yes." The lump in his throat swelled so large he couldn't speak.

"You have others here who love you. Kahlia and Pono, Elizabeth, your staff. Glory loves you, too."

He shook his head, but he couldn't bring himself to argue with her. Not now.

"Love is what really matters, Jared. If you don't have love, you don't have anything. Nothing can replace it, nothing can change it. It's always there, forever." Her eyelids drooped closed and for a moment he thought she slept. "Get my Bible, Jared. There on the stand."

He lifted the worn book into his hands.

"I Corinthians 13. Will you read it for me?"

He flipped through the dog-eared pages, found the chapter. It bore many lines, notes on the sides, dates marked in red, a testament to her use of the book.

"Will you read it to me?"

Jared began reciting the familiar words. He'd memorized them years earlier. But now they seemed more pertinent, more alive. Especially when he came to the fifth verse.

"'Love is never haughty or selfish or rude. Love does not demand its own way. It is not irritable or touchy. It does not hold grudges and will hardly even notice when others do it wrong.'"

Sister's eyes were closed, but a beatific smile lit up her face.

"'If you love someone you will be loyal to him no matter what the cost. You will always believe in him, always expect the best of him, and always stand your ground in defending him,'" she recited.

Eyes closed, she continued through to the end of the verse until the last one. There she stopped, sighed.

"'There are three things that remain—faith, hope and love—and the greatest of these is love,'" he finished for her.

"Yes. The greatest. Choose love, Jared. Choose the best." Her fingers gave his the barest squeeze before she drew one last breath.

Then she was gone.

Elizabeth hurried into the room as the machine signaled Sister Phil's passing. Jared flipped it and the others off, watched as she moved to the side of her cousin.

"She's gone now, Elizabeth," he murmured.

"I know. But I want to sit with her a minute." She blinked through her tears. "Could you tell the others, please? Glory, too. I just saw her heading down to the beach with her lunch."

"I'll tell her." Jared waited a moment then left the little cottage he'd come to for solace so often. He hated the task that lay before him, most of all he hated having to tell Glory. So he started at Agapé, let the staff know.

Then he walked toward the precipice overlooking the beach. She was in the water, happily paddling through it, the sun tinting her hair gold.

Sighing, Jared climbed down the steps, sank onto the sand to wait for her.

As soon as she saw him she hurried out of the water. "What's wrong?"

He rose, handed her the towel she'd dropped on the sand. When she didn't take it, he wrapped it around her like a sarong.

"Sister Phil," she whispered. Jagged misery washed over her beautiful features. "Oh, no." Tears formed on her lashes, dropped onto her cheeks. She made no attempt to hide them. Instead, she laid her head on his chest and wept.

"She died happy, Glory." He wrapped his arms around her waist and held on.

"I know."

"We'll miss her."

"So much. At the end, you were with her?"

"Yes. She asked me to read a passage from her Bible then she took over, quoting it from memory. She wanted to go home, her real home."

"She's not suffering anymore. That's good." Glory searched his face. "I'm glad you got to speak to her again."

"So am I." She felt so precious in his arms, delicate yet infinitely strong. He could not make himself let go.

"Jared?" she whispered when long moments had passed.

"Yes?"

"Will you kiss me?"

"Yes." He bent his head, placed his lips against hers and kissed her as if she was the most precious thing in the world. He could not deny his heart what it craved most.

Glory tried with all her heart to step away, to break the embrace she'd longed for. But her body had a mind of its own and her arms clung to him, holding him next to her heart. The nerves that always attacked whenever he was around dissipated into nothingness as she wound a hand in his hair, drowning in the tenderness he exuded.

For her.

His kiss went on so long she prayed it would never end. But then her breath caught as he drew back slightly, peered down into her face. She felt so alive.

"Glory—"

She shook her head, laid her palm over his lips.

"I need to say something."

Glory whispered a prayer for help.

"I love you, Jared," she murmured, studying her hand splayed against his chest. "I never meant for it to happen, I have no idea why God allowed it, nor do I know what to do with it. I have to go back to Tiska, keep my promise. But my heart will stay here, with you."

Jared grasped her wrists, drew them down so she had to step back, away from him. A hundred emotions chased across his face but she could only make out three of them: wonder, regret and rejection.

"Don't love me," he begged.

She studied him for a moment before finally asking the one question that plagued her.

"What's wrong? Do you have any feelings for me?"

He closed his eyes.

"It doesn't matter what I feel, Glory."

"Of course it does." She gulped. Unless—"You don't love me," she murmured, a wave of desolation swamping her. "I see."

"No, you don't see!" He pushed the bedraggled strands of hair off her face, cupped her chin in his fingers and pressed one hard firm kiss against her lips.

Glory didn't know what to make of it, how to interpret the anger that filled the air around them with a palpable tension.

"You don't understand at all." He brushed his thumb against the cleft in her chin. "When I look at you I see light and beauty, all the good things I wish were in my own life. You give love so generously, Glory. Sometimes I catch myself craving to be nearer you, to bask in the joy you spread around, to let it wash away the hurt."

Her heart sang.

"I wish we could build a world together, that I could give you everything your heart desires, make you happy."

"You already have," she told him, unshed tears dragging at her words.

"No, I haven't. Because I can't." He dragged a hand through his hair. "There can never be anything between us, Glory. Never."

The words grated across her nerves, leaving her raw and bleeding.

"You can let go of your bitterness, with God's help.

I know you can, Jared. We can both trust Him to lead us to a future together."

"Trust God?" He barked a laugh. "No. I won't trust Him again. I can't."

"So it's about Diana. You're still in love with her."

"Diana was my wife and I did love her very much. Some part of me will always love her. But she's gone now and my heart is filled with you. Not loving you— that's like not breathing. I can't stop. I don't want to."

"I feel the same. So tell me why we can't have a future," she whispered, fear dragging at her heart.

"Because you deserve happiness, a loving family, children." He met her gaze, his face gray and tortured. "I can't give you that."

He was trying to tell her something, but she couldn't understand.

"I can't have any more children, Glory. I caught the mumps after my son was born. Nicholas was the only child I'll ever have."

Relief swamped her.

"I'm so sorry, but Agapé is brimming with children. The world is teeming with kids who want to be loved, Jared." She touched his face, forced him to look at her. "I don't care about the biology. Our love will grow strong enough to share with any child we choose."

"It won't be enough," he insisted. "In six months, a year—somewhere down the road—you'll look at me and hate the fact that you can't have your own child. You deserve that and I can't give it to you. I won't put you through that, Glory."

She stepped back, repelled by the hard way he pushed love aside because it didn't conform to what he wanted.

"Is that how Diana felt? Did she want to leave you, end your marriage because you couldn't give her more children?" She shook her head. "I've heard Kahlia talk about her. I know how much she loved you."

"That was different. She had Nicholas."

"So you'll run away again," she whispered. "You'll turn your back on any possibility that you don't have the answers because you're afraid to risk getting hurt."

"I'm not doing that."

"Sure you are. It's your pattern, Jared. It's what you do—run from the hard parts in life. Refuse to push past the pain and the fear because it's easier to wallow in your misery." She had to try, one last time. "But if you'd just let go, release your control to God and let Him get you through it, you'd be free to face whatever He has next."

"What do you think that is, Glory? Another child suffering, another kid disfigured?" Fury banked in his eyes as he lowered his voice. "I can't."

"Then you're right." She stepped back. "You are not the man I need. I have to go back, keep my promise. But if you'd only let God show us what He has in store, we could have worked it out."

"I told you, I can't love you."

"No. What you've told me is that you won't. You had a choice, Jared. You pushed me away." She picked up her bag, slipped on her sandals and left, hurrying back to her cottage, anxious to get behind closed doors before the tears fell.

Only in the shower did Glory finally allow hot tears to mingle with the water cascading over her head. She had never felt more alone.

Please don't desert me now, she prayed soundlessly. *I need You to show me how to go on. How to live without him. Please show me Your will.*

Her only response was the sound of the beeper she'd left on the table.

Chapter Thirteen

Sister Philomena's service overflowed Agapé's small chapel and spilled to the outdoors. Everyone who had been touched by her wanted to be there. Pono created special areas of peace and tranquillity in the gardens where the sun and ocean breezes mingled to carry the fragrance of love Heavenward.

Jared had come because it was his duty, because he owed it to Elizabeth. But he didn't want to be here. He'd already bid farewell to the woman who'd been his best friend for the past three years. He didn't need the formality of a funeral.

Besides, he was too conscious of Glory seated next to him. Coolly composed and classically beautiful, she wore the dress she'd bought that day in Honolulu and a big sun hat. Philomena would have loved it. But to Jared it brought back too many memories of a time he would always cherish.

Since that day on the beach, Glory spoke to him politely, but only when necessary. She worked the schedule so they were seldom in the wards together. When a consult was necessary, she got to the point, heard his opinion and escaped as quickly as she could.

Not that Jared blamed her. In some ways it helped make his decision easier to adhere to. But it hurt. Mostly because she'd lost that inner glow he'd come to associate with dear Dr. Glory.

"She was my cousin, my friend, my partner, my sister in Christ. I will miss you, Philomena." Elizabeth stopped to regain her composure then addressed her audience. "This mission, Agapé, is a testament to the love she believed was the only way to show God's true personality. I hope you'll work with me to ensure its continued success. Let us pray."

Jared stuck it out through the burial service, through the lunch in the garden, through the inevitable chatter, glad that for once no emergencies marred the memories of their beloved Sister.

But he itched to leave.

In fact, Jared wanted to run as far and as fast as he could go.

Glory's diagnosis had been right on. He was afraid. Afraid of staying the way he was, afraid of changing and losing again, afraid of putting his trust in the place he'd found so sadly lacking. Because the truth was, keeping Viktor behind bars hadn't appeased his heart.

Glory had been right there, too.

"This came for you." Leilani handed him a small envelope. It bore the imprint of Halawa prison. "Can't you let it go, Jared? Just for tonight."

He took the letter, slid it into his jacket pocket. "I have a meeting. I can't reschedule it again."

"But today is—"

"Thank you, Leilani. I know what today is." He turned his back, escaped as soon as he could and sought solace in the empty wards.

Jared sat, slit the envelope, pulled out a single sheet of paper.

Several times I've requested a meeting with you but have not made any progress. So I must write because I cannot continue with this burden any longer. I must do as my Lord requires and apologize. I know this is not enough. I stole innocent lives. Nothing I can do or say could ever make my actions right. But God asks me to try.

So many times I think of our two sons, two young innocent children who died too early. Perhaps they play together in Heaven, perhaps they are even friends. I pray so. I pray my son never knows the actions of his father, that he never learns of my sins. I cannot disregard that two people died because of my anger. I accept my guilt. But I also accept my son's death was not your fault. You are innocent, Jared. I hope that someday you will accept my apology. I expect nothing. My crime was very great indeed. It will require my life to atone.

I pray God's healing on you.
Viktor

Jared crushed the paper into a tiny ball. But then he smoothed it out again, reread the words so carefully penned.

You are innocent.

Hardly.

I pray God's healing on you.

"Are you sad?" Fingers that had once been chubby and healthy, now thin and too bony, patted his arm awkwardly.

Bennie.

"Are you sad about your boy?" he asked, pushing himself into Jared's lap. His one chubby arm looped itself around his neck, drawing his head down.

Jared gazed into the big brown eyes so like Nicholas's, felt the silken brush of the dark-brown strands against his chin, the warmth of the small body snuggling itself against him. He had to close his eyes as the smell—that combination of sweaty little boy and fresh bath powder—assailed his nostrils.

Dear God! I hurt so much.

Bennie touched his cheek, stared at the wet spot on his finger.

"I can pray for Jesus to make you better," he whispered so quietly the other children filing into the room couldn't possibly hear. "Do you want me to?"

What else could he say?

"Okay," Jared murmured.

"You have to close your eyes." Bennie waited till his lashes drooped. Satisfied, he began to pray. "This doctor has a hurt, God. He needs Your good medicine. Can You get him some? Please?" He opened one eye, smiled at Jared. "Amen."

"Thank you, Bennie. That was very kind of you."

"Welcome." He slid down, paused, then beckoned for Jared to lean down. "Glory Mom is going to make me better," he whispered, his eyes dancing.

"Is she?"

"Yes. She promised. Then I won't hurt anymore."

"That's good. Do you mind if I look at your shoulder now?"

"No." Bennie backed away, his face changing. "It hurts when you look."

"I promise I won't touch it. I'll just look. Okay?"

It took several minutes for Bennie to make his decision, but finally he undid his top and allowed Jared to undo the bandage.

It took every control Jared possessed not to show his emotion. The wound was blistered, infected and in a terrible state, far worse than he'd imagined. Who had let it get so bad?

He had. He'd avoided Bennie because when he looked at him, he saw Nicholas. But Jared would never have allowed anyone to hurt *his* child this way.

Shame pierced his very soul.

Oh, God, help me!

"What are you doing, Jared?" Glory loomed above them, her eyes chilly.

"Just taking a look at Bennie's shoulder." He waved the nurse over for fresh gauze, rewound the bandage as gently as he could. "Thank you for showing me, Bennie. I hope I didn't hurt you."

"Nope." Bennie pressed against Glory's leg, found her hand with his good one. "Is it time to make me better now?"

"Not just yet, sweetheart," she murmured. "It's almost time for bed, though. I think Kahlia's got a really good story tonight."

He gazed longingly at the corner where the children gathered to hear a nighttime story.

"Are you coming?"

"In a minute. I need to talk to Dr. Jared first."

"Okay." Bennie held out his hand toward Jared. "Good night." He solemnly shook hands.

"Sleep well." As the boy hurried to the story corner, Jared studied Glory. "He told me you promised to make him better."

"I did."

"How are you going to do that?"

"I've been studying the videos of the procedure. I've gotten very good at it. In a week, maybe two, I'll try it on Bennie."

He blanched.

"You can't! You don't know enough. What if something goes wrong?"

"It already has," she reminded him softly. "A little boy is suffering needlessly. I'm not going to stand by if there's something I can do to prevent it."

"Glory, please, don't do this." He grabbed his vibrating pager, checked the message. The prison chaplain was on line two. "I've got to take this call. Look, don't do anything until we talk again."

"And when will that be?" she demanded. "You don't seem to have much time to spend here anymore."

"Just don't do anything. Please?" He took her arm, led her out of the ward. "If it goes wrong, Bennie won't have another chance. The procedure can only be done once."

His beeper went off again.

"Go," she ordered.

"Will you promise not to do anything tonight? Please?" He touched her cheek, let his hand drop away when she shifted out of reach. The beeper shook again. "Please, I'm begging you. Wait."

Finally she nodded.

"But not forever, Jared. I only have a couple of months left here. I don't intend to waste my time."

"Thank you."

He raced down the hall to the front desk.

"What is the urgency, Leilani?" he demanded.

"The prison chaplain says Viktor insists he'll kill himself if he doesn't get a chance to talk to you. He's on line one."

Talk to him? Have a conversation with the murderer? Wouldn't it be better to let him die?

This doctor needs Your good medicine.

"I don't know what I can do but get him to hold till I can pick up in my office."

Leilani nodded. "Will do. I'll be praying, boss."

"You do that."

It felt good to be free.

"Viktor says to thank you."

"I should be thanking him. Tell the warden I concur with the board. Get him some help."

Jared snapped his cell phone closed, sat in his car and listened to the surf pound the rocks beyond. He felt like those rocks—bruised and battered but strong enough to face the future.

He needed to see Glory.

The little beach park was empty, so it took only seconds to turn the car around, head back to Agapé. But the closer he got the more Jared noticed a strange light in the sky. His nose caught a scent.

Smoke!

He drove as fast as he dared, got as far as the barricade. Smoke poured from the rear of the building. Ambulances loaded patients while Leilani directed operations. Board members who'd come for the funeral comforted those who needed it. Even Kahlia and Pono pitched in.

But he couldn't see her.

"Where's Glory, Leilani?"

"I don't know. We were helping the kids in Bennie's ward get out. I didn't see her after that." She answered his unspoken question. "So far no one's been injured, Jared. So far."

Except for Glory. Terror grabbed his heart. He couldn't breathe.

Choose love, Jared. Choose the best.

"I love her," he whispered to the only One who heard. "I love her so much. Don't take her away. Not Glory."

God's will?

It had to be. He understood that now. Not just with Viktor but with Glory, too.

"Your will be done, Lord. Your will."

A hand closed around his arm. He turned, saw Elizabeth, her face dirty, her hair askew.

"Glory's inside," the older woman croaked. "They won't let me go in after her. Glory's inside and she's going to die."

"No, she isn't." With faith filling his heart, Jared clung to trust. "Pray, Elizabeth. Get the children taken care of and then pray."

He found the fire chief.

"I've got to get in there. One of my doctors was caught inside with a little boy. I have to get them out."

"Too much smoke. I've had four men injured. I won't send in any more. You'll never find her."

"I'll find her. I know this place like the back of my hand. You keep your men safe. But I'm going in."

It took persuasion before they allowed him to put on a suit. He was ready when a volunteer fireman offered to brave the smoke one more time to save two lives.

"Thank you."

They worked their way from the kitchen upward, using the inflammable areas of stainless steel to shield them from the heat. A loud creak echoed down the hallway then a piece of debris tumbled from the wall, struck his partner. He went down with a crash but signaled he was okay. But his mask was cracked. There was no way he could go inside.

"Go back, go back," Jared ordered. "Wait outside. If I need you I'll call."

Ignoring the protests, he forged ahead, unable to see anything until he was on top of it.

"Oh, God, protect them," he prayed as he felt his way along the wall. "Keep them safe, shield them."

He came up against something hard and metal—a cart for bringing meals to the ward. It was blocking the door. He rolled it free then used it as a barrier, pushing it in front of him as he called her name.

"Glory! Where are you?"

He was almost at the end of the ward when he heard the noise.

"Bennie?"

"We're here, Dr. Jared. Glory Mom is hurt."

"I choose love," Jared repeated. "I choose love. Not fear, not hatred. Love."

Then aloud, "Talk to me, Bennie. I have to follow your voice because I can't see anything."

"We're in the story corner, under the big rug. Glory Mom said God would keep us safe here. We couldn't get out."

"We're getting out now. Is Glory awake?"

"No. She hurt her head and then she went to sleep."

"Okay, just wait a minute until I figure this out."

He'd have to put them in the cart, close the side and wheel them to the stairs. There was no other way.

"Okay, Bennie, in a minute I'm going to lift the blanket up. You know that big thing they bring ice cream in sometimes?"

"Uh-huh."

"You and Glory are going to ride inside it. Okay?"

"Will it be hot? I don't like hot."

"I know, son. And it might be hot for a little while. But I promise you, Bennie, I'll get you out of here. Do you trust me?"

A pause.

"Glory Mom said I could always trust you. She said God would help you help me."

"She was right."

What a woman!

"Okay, are you ready? Here we go." He peeled back the blanket and almost fainted when he saw the singed hair framing Glory's beloved face.

"Okay, first I have to take Glory. Put this over your mouth." He handed Bennie a towel. "Stay there, Bennie. I'll be right back."

Quickly he lifted Glory in his arms. The gash on her

head was bleeding and she was very pale, but as he set her inside the cart she came to.

"Jared?"

"Stay still. I'm going to get Bennie." He kissed her on the temple, slid down the metal sides of the cart then went back to get the little boy. There was no other way than to set him in her lap, not an easy feat given the size constrictions.

"It's too tight. I don't like this." Bennie began to cry when a loud bang echoed through the room.

"Hang on to Glory, Bennie. We're going for your ride now." Jared closed the sides and began pushing, but passage grew difficult as ceiling litter blocked the wheels. He touched the radio. "I've got them. I'm coming back out. Meet me at the stairwell."

"Roger that."

When it was too difficult to push, he pulled. And when that didn't work he manhandled the unit. Bennie's yells let him know he at least was all right. Glory didn't respond.

"Oh, God, help me," he begged. "I have to get them out of here. This is a place for saving lives, a place of love. Agapé means love. Don't let it become a place of death."

A draft of air pushed through the room suddenly, clearing the smoke from in front of him, allowing Jared to see the IV pole that blocked the path. He tossed it aside.

"Thank You, Lord. Just a little bit farther."

But the same draft that had cleared the smoke now fanned the flames. The temperature soared. They had to get out fast. Bennie was screaming.

Jared reached the door. It opened. Three men pulled

him and the cart through the door then slammed it shut. Immediately chatter on the radio ordered the hoses on this section of the building.

Jared opened the door of the cart.

"Come on, Bennie. Time to get out now."

"But Glory Mom. I want Glory Mom!"

"She's coming, too, don't worry."

A pair of arms lifted the boy from him and passed him to the next man in the line. Jared bent, eased Glory from the lifesaving metal.

"I'll carry her myself," he insisted. The men stood aside so he could walk down the now-cleared stairs. Jared carried her toward the ambulance. "Head injury," he gasped.

"We've got her, Doc. You sit down and catch your breath."

But he didn't. Instead, Jared hovered helplessly as they took her vital signs, checked her body for other wounds.

Finally her lovely eyes opened.

"Jared?" she croaked, wincing as she tried to speak.

"Hi."

She tried to sit up. "Bennie, where's Bennie?"

"Doc got you both out," the paramedic told her. "Good thing, too. That end of the building is pretty bad."

Her eyes widened in shock.

Jared took her hand. "It's okay," he whispered. "God protected us. All of us."

"God?" Her eyes darkened to the forest shade he loved. "Really?"

He nodded. "I'm sorry I wasn't here. I had to get some help for Viktor."

"Help Viktor?"

"Look, Doc, we have to get her arm stitched up. You two can talk later."

Arm? He saw the stain, the gash. How had he missed that?

"Take her," he told the attendant. But first he bent, brushed his lips against hers. "I love you, Glory."

She didn't respond, but Jared knew the truth. She loved him. It would be enough, for now.

He watched them load her, saw the blood.

Glory winced, then fainted.

"Oh, God, please, not Glory, too."

His will.

Chapter Fourteen

"Someone to see you, Dr. Cranbrook."

"Bennie!" She'd been in hospital four days and hadn't seen him once. The relief of knowing he was all right took her breath away. "Hello, sweetheart. How are you?"

"Good. Are you good, too?"

She laughed. "Very good, darling."

Glory couldn't stop herself from glancing at his shoulder. Of course, it was covered by his hospital gown at the moment, but she knew the unsightly damage that lay beneath. Maybe now that Jared—maybe.

She was so tired of the maybes.

"I brought you a letter." He slid it out from under his leg where he sat in the wheelchair. "Here."

He thrust it at her then asked the nurse to wheel him to the hospital window where he could look outside, as if he knew she'd want privacy.

Glory ripped open the envelope, pulled out the single sheet.

Darling Glory,

I'm going crazy. Why won't you see me? I love you. I always will. I have so much to share with you.

Please let me visit.

Jared

Tears threatened as she folded the paper into the pages of her Bible. But she couldn't weaken, she wouldn't.

"Bennie, have you seen any of the other children?"

"Uh-huh. Some of us are going back tomorrow. A big man told me."

"Back?" She frowned. "But—"

"Hello, dear." Elizabeth stood in the doorway. "You look better today. How's your arm?"

"It's fine." She ignored the sting of pain. "Elizabeth, how is it possible for some of the children to go back?"

"Well, thanks to many volunteers, we did a massive cleanup. Two of the wards are virtually untouched. We'll begin using those tomorrow. The rest needs work, but the board is fully committed to getting Agapé up and running as soon as possible."

"What caused the problem? Why didn't the sprinklers stay on?"

"Some malfunction in the pump. I'm not exactly sure of the details, but it's been rectified. We're having additional fire-suppression equipment installed today."

"Everything's moving so fast."

"It seems slow to me." Elizabeth bent to speak to Bennie just before he hugged Glory. His nurse wheeled him away. "Your head, Glory. Have things straightened out?"

Her confusion and memory lapse scared Glory, but slowly everything was righting itself.

"I'll be fine. Back to work in a day or two, I think."

"I don't want you back there until you're fully healed."

"Elizabeth?"

"Yes, dear."

She struggled to say the words, knowing how difficult her request would be.

"I want to go home," she murmured.

"You will, dear. Just be patient for a couple more days."

"No, I mean my real home. The North. They have no one, Elizabeth. They need me. Agapé doesn't. God's will is for me to serve in the North and I can't turn my back on that."

"Have you really prayed about this?"

"I've tried."

"Keep trying, Glory. And open your heart to His answers."

"Thanks for coming. And for the flowers. Thank the others for me, will you?"

Elizabeth fluttered her hand and walked out.

The world had never seemed so bleak. Glory picked up her Bible and tried to read the words but she couldn't see through the tears. Everything she loved was here, Bennie, Jared—but God was asking her to give up her own desires, to serve him.

She fought an inner battle until finally she surrendered.

"Not my will but Yours," she whispered.

At last blessed sleep brought her peace.

Jared stood on the precipice overlooking the cove and watched the sun crawl over the horizon.

Easter morning.

In the weeks since the fire he'd had little time to ponder the changes in his life. But this morning he'd risen early especially to do that, and he'd never been more thankful.

Bennie's surgery was first of many he'd done in the hospital where Glory had been taken. The boy was healing well. In a year it would be hard to distinguish him from any other boy his age. There'd been many more, each one a joy and accomplishment that fed his soul, kept him focused on God, the giver of life. Not that there hadn't been complications, there had. But Jared was learning to do his part and leave the rest to God.

Viktor was doing well under treatment. Jared's anger, the bitterness—all were gone through the mercy of God.

But Glory would not be swayed from her intention to return home. She treated every day as if it might be her last. She continued to keep the children busy, planned events for them, cheered them through their treatments, but with a detachment that was completely unlike her usual self.

Even with Jared she was distant, though he'd told her over and over how much he loved her, longed for her to believe that somehow God would work it out, that they would be together. She simply smiled and made an excuse to get away. She was biding her time.

Jared would gladly go north to be with her, except he belonged at Agapé and he knew it. This was where God wanted to use him. He could not disobey. At the same time he recognized Glory's loyalty to her mother, the people she loved and the job she'd embraced. God had called her, too.

So he waited for God to do His will, shared as much of the island as he could with Glory. In those precious moments when her mask slipped, she returned his embrace, kissed him with heartfelt fervor and told him how much she loved him.

But they both knew time was running out.

Jared had clung to his trust in God, waited for an answer. But he'd found none.

That's why he'd come here to pray.

He praised God for his mercy and gift of sacrifice then asked for what he wanted most.

"I want to marry her. I don't care about having children or where we live as long as we both serve You. Your will be done."

Like a dart of fire a voice exploded inside him.

Propose.

He couldn't do that. Glory was leaving.

Propose. The word kept singing into his brain.

Jared was God's servant. He'd said he'd obey. He would propose and leave the rest up to God.

In the distance two whales surfaced, blew air out then dived.

"Jared?"

Glory stood behind him, her short wispy hair bathed in the golden beams of dawn.

The fire had changed all of them.

"Good morning, beloved." He rose, slipped his arms around her waist and kissed her, savoring the sweetness of this moment.

"Elizabeth wants to see us."

"Okay. But first I have to ask you something."

Her eyes appeared twice as large with her hair so short.

"What?"

"I love you. I would die for you, Glory. You are my life, the best part of me. You are the woman God sent to bring me out of the darkness and into His glorious light."

She lifted one small hand, touched his face. "Jared."

"Will you marry me, GloryAnn Cranbrook?"

"But—"

"I don't know how, I don't know when, but I believe that somehow God will honor the love He's given us. Will you marry me?"

Her troubled gaze studied him for a long time. "We can't."

He tilted her chin, touched his lips to hers.

"When did you stop trusting God, GloryAnn?"

Tears welled.

"I trust Him. With my life." A tremulous smile transformed her face. "I will marry you, Jared. Soon, I hope."

They kissed, sealing their pledge as the sun rose to its full glory and Japanese White-eyes began their dawn songs of tinkling praise and joy. Land breezes surrounded them with fragrant white ginger in celebration.

"We have God on our side, Glory. Let's go hear what Elizabeth wants."

"Yes."

Jared smiled as he took her hand, drew her with him toward Agapé.

They found Elizabeth in the chapel, arranging flowers as she hummed an Easter song.

"Ah, there you are. Let's all sit, shall we?"

He and Glory took the front pew. Elizabeth sat behind them. They turned to face her.

"I have some news for you, dear ones. Do you remember a board member named Harmon? He visited little Bennie in the hospital several times after his surgery. I think he even stopped by to say hello to you, Glory."

"Yes, he did."

"Harmon discovered he has a connection with Bennie."

Glory's body jerked. Jared leaned closer.

"Trust, remember?" He nodded at Elizabeth. "Please continue."

"Bennie's father saved Harmon's life when they were both on a peace-keeping mission. When Harmon learned Bennie's father and the rest of the family had died, he wanted to do something to honor his friend."

"So he's going to buy Agapé that new machine it needs," Jared guessed.

"No." Elizabeth's brown eyes danced. "When he learned why Glory is so insistent on returning to the Arctic, he called together a bunch of his friends. Corporate sponsors have raised enough funds to build and furnish a health-care center in Tiska. They've had plans drawn up and approved for the Cranbrook Center. Construction will begin as soon as possible."

Glory burst into tears.

"It gets better. Two young men, sons of missionaries your parents supported overseas, feel God has called them to Tiska to serve as community doctors. They've agreed to accept Harmon's son as a third partner on condition that, from time to time, you return to give them a break."

"They don't want me to go back?"

"I think three doctors are enough for your town, aren't they?"

"Abundantly beyond what I could ask or think. I'll gladly help out whenever they need me. Thank you,

Elizabeth." Glory hugged her benefactor. "And please thank Harmon, too. It will be a wonderful tribute."

"You'll get to thank him yourself. He's flying in this afternoon."

She sniffed, patted away her tears. "I can't believe this."

Jared wrapped his arms around her and lifted her off her feet as he swung her around.

"Believe it because we are getting married. I love you."

"I love you, too." He kissed her until childish giggles broke them apart.

"Come on, darling. The children are waiting for their egg hunt."

She wiped her eyes, gave him a brave smile and laid her hand in his.

"Then let's not disappoint the children."

They'd chosen an egg hunt specifically as an illustration that would help the children understand the real meaning of Easter. Glory finished the story then encouraged each child to open their egg.

"I hope you'll always remember the special gift God gave us at Easter."

Bennie crawled up on her lap.

"What about your egg?" Bennie asked, big brown eyes shining.

She knelt, cuddled him close, the precious child she loved more than her own life.

"I guess I don't have one."

"Yes, you do. There." He bent, pointed under her chair.

The "egg" was a handmade concoction of papiermâché painted with soft pastels and tied with a silver ribbon. Her name glittered on top.

"Did you make this?" she asked, twisting and turning it to get a better look.

"No." He shook his head but his gaze swiveled to meet Jared's. "He did."

"You're not the only one who can do crafts," Jared teased, a lambent glow lighting his blue eyes. "Open it, Glory."

She untied the ribbon, traced the crack and gently pressed the egg apart. Inside, on a bed of plastic grass, sat a glittering engagement ring.

"Happy Easter, Glory." Jared leaned forward to kiss her, laughed when Bennie insisted he needed a kiss, too.

One of the nurses shepherded the other children out of the room, leaving them alone.

Jared slid the band on her finger. "If you don't like it I could—"

"Dream on. You're not getting this back and you're not reneging on marriage, Jared Steele, so don't even think about it."

"Who's thinking?" He glanced around the ward, made a face. "This place isn't exactly romantic. Can we get out of here?"

"In a second." Glory called Bennie over, showed him her ring and explained they were to be married.

"Then Dr. Jared will be my daddy," he whooped and took off racing across the room to spread the good news.

"We could adopt him, Glory." Jared took her hand, led her outside, down to the beach. "After we're married we could adopt him as our son."

"I'd like that."

They sealed the deal with a kiss.

"You seem pensive. Is anything wrong?"

"Well, there is something that's been bothering me."

"Tell me," he encouraged, wrapping his arm around her waist as they watched darkness fall.

"I was thinking about our wedding."

"I've never been to the Arctic. Will you show me the sights?"

"What about the children? They should be present. They are a part of us. How can I choose between here and there?"

"Why do you have to?" He touched her nose, traced her lips. "We'll have two weddings. One here, one there."

"Two? But that's hardly usual."

Jared burst out laughing. "My darling Glory, there is nothing usual about us. We're hardly typical. Arctic and tropical."

"I like husband and wife better," she told him.

"Me, too."

Epilogue

The wedding of Drs. Jared Steele and GloryAnn Cranbrook took place in Tiska at the end of June, when the sun forgot to go to sleep and the cold white world withdrew to make room for new life.

The bride wore a traditional Inuit wedding costume. So did her friends and the little boy who preceded the wedding party down the aisle. Chuckles erupted when Bennie explained exactly how Arctic wildflowers should be scattered.

Pono gave the bride away while Kahlia tended Bennie. Harmon and Elizabeth ensured all the guests enjoyed a sumptuous buffet.

A second wedding took place a week later, at Agapé's beach. The bride wore a plain white silk dress that grazed her bare toes. The groom sported a colorful Hawaiian shirt identical to Bennie's. Glory chose Elizabeth and Leilani as attendants. Bennie stood by Jared.

The entire hospital was invited to a traditional luau feast.

It was after dark, while the music still whispered on

the wind and the children were coaxed to their beds, that Jared and Glory finally left the party. They were in their car ready to drive away when Elizabeth appeared.

"I have a gift for you."

"Elizabeth, you've already given us so much. We can't accept anything more."

"It's not from me," she explained. "You'll have to come with me to see it."

So they followed her to Sister Phil's cottage. A painting sat on the sofa.

"She did it herself. She made me promise that when you got married, I'd give it to you."

"She knew?" Glory traced the top half of the painting, her fingertips grazing over silvery white mounds of snow bowing to the midnight-blue of an Arctic night.

"She knew." Jared smiled at the bottom scene of a beach, "their" beach, peeking through the fronds of a palm tree while whitecaps rippled over the sea beyond.

"There's a note," Elizabeth explained. She held out a sheet of paper on which a faint spidery hand had written.

God created individuals with special abilities not to further their own plans, but to make His plan complete. When you can't hear His voice, trust His heart.

They turned to thank her but Elizabeth had left them alone.

"We'll build our home around it," Glory whispered as she leaned her head against his shoulder and remembered the wonderful woman who'd started the legacy they would now continue.

"God and His will," Jared agreed. "What could be better?"

Dear Reader,

Aloha!

Welcome to Hawaii. I chose this setting for the first book in my new series PENNIES FROM HEAVEN because it is so beautiful and because beauty often hides pain. I hope you enjoyed *Healing Tides*. Jared and GloryAnn's story is one of change. They came from two different worlds to Agapé, a place of love. Their searches and struggles are not unlike our own as we learn to relinquish our will to God and understand that He has a much broader vision.

I hope you'll return next month for a visit to a homeless shelter in Chicago. But as you'll see, Hearts Haven is a lot more than a place to sleep.

As always, I wish you love, peace and joy. But most of all I wish for you the certain knowledge that you are the beloved child of the most high King, that you are more precious to Him than all the gold in Heaven.

I'd love to hear from you. Contact me at www.loisricher.com, loisricher@yahoo.com or write Box 639, Nipawin, Saskatchewan, Canada S0E 1E0.

Blessings,

Lois
Richer

QUESTIONS FOR DISCUSSION

1. Glory's parents were missionaries. Discuss the role of a missionary as well as some of the difficulties missionaries' children face.

2. Is revenge the same as justice? Give examples where the two might overlap in your own life.

3. Sister Philomena was a pivotal character in both Glory's and Jared's faith journey. How? Did you think of her as a mentor? Consider those in your own life who have cheered you on, supported you or taught you new ways to resolve issues. How can you be such a mentor to someone else?

4. Forgiveness is difficult for most people, especially when one has lost a lot. Often we cannot forgive until we've glimpsed our own forgiveness from God. Are there people you feel you can never forgive? Are there people you feel will never forgive you? Share ways of coaxing our hearts to see that getting and giving forgiveness is a way to heal ourselves.

5. God's will is as hard for some to discover as it is for others to obey. What suggestions would you offer to someone who seeks to understand what God wants them to do?

6. Is it possible to enjoy not forgiving someone? Share reasons behind your thoughts and ways to avoid this trap.

7. Glory loved Bennie in spite of his injuries. Suggest ways we can escape our personal biases and allow ourselves to show our love to others in a true missionary sense.

8. Elizabeth's foundation reaches out to help women with potential. Do you know of such a foundation? Discuss ways individual women of faith can nurture and support young ladies who struggle to fulfill their potential.

9. Search for Old Testament passages about punishment for those who broke Jewish laws. Do you think they were too harsh? Consider ways we, as busy parents, can be certain our children learn responsibility for their actions in the global community.

10. Agapé is a fictional mission but there are many real ones around the world working to help the needy, often struggling to fund their efforts. Study a mission. Discuss ways to choose a place to support financially. Contrast the benefits of regular support for such efforts against emergency giving for projects like tsunamis and earthquakes.

INTRODUCING

Love Inspired.

HISTORICAL

A NEW TWO-BOOK SERIES.

Every month, acclaimed
inspirational authors
will bring you engaging stories
rich with romance, adventure
and faith set in a variety
of vivid historical times.

History begins on **February 12**
wherever you buy books.

Steeple
Hill®

www.SteepleHill.com

REQUEST YOUR FREE BOOKS!

2 FREE INSPIRATIONAL NOVELS
PLUS 2
FREE
MYSTERY GIFTS

Love Inspired.

YES! Please send me 2 FREE Love Inspired® novels and my 2 FREE mystery gifts. After receiving them, if I don't wish to receive any more books, I can return the shipping statement marked "cancel." If I don't cancel, I will receive 4 brand-new novels every month and be billed just $3.99 per book in the U.S., or $4.74 per book in Canada, plus 25¢ shipping and handling per book and applicable taxes, if any*. That's a savings of 20% off the cover price! I understand that accepting the 2 free books and gifts places me under no obligation to buy anything. I can always return a shipment and cancel at any time. Even if I never buy another book from Steeple Hill, the two free books and gifts are mine to keep forever.

113 IDN EF26 313 IDN EF27

Name	(PLEASE PRINT)	
Address		Apt. #
City	State/Prov.	Zip/Postal Code

Signature (if under 18, a parent or guardian must sign)

Order online at www.LoveInspiredBooks.com

Or mail to Steeple Hill Reader Service™:

IN U.S.A.: P.O. Box 1867, Buffalo, NY 14240-1867
IN CANADA: P.O. Box 609, Fort Erie, Ontario L2A 5X3

Not valid to current Love Inspired subscribers.

Want to try two free books from another series?
Call 1-800-873-8635 or visit www.morefreebooks.com

* Terms and prices subject to change without notice. NY residents add applicable sales tax. Canadian residents will be charged applicable provincial taxes and GST. This offer is limited to one order per household. All orders subject to approval. Credit or debit balances in a customer's account(s) may be offset by any other outstanding balance owed by or to the customer. Please allow 4 to 6 weeks for delivery.

Your Privacy: Steeple Hill is committed to protecting your privacy. Our Privacy Policy is available online at www.eHarlequin.com or upon request from the Reader Service. From time to time we make our lists of customers available to reputable firms who may have a product or service of interest to you. If you would prefer we not share your name and address, please check here. ☐

LIREG07

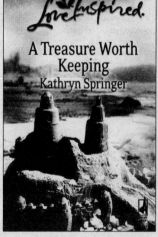

Love Inspired™

Spending the summer in tiny, idyllic Cooper's Landing sounded perfect to play-it-safe teacher Evie McBride. She'd read, relax and help out in her dad's antique shop. So how did she end up tutoring Sam Cutter's troubled teenage niece? Especially since Sam's handsome face and sense of adventure didn't give her a moment's peace....

Look for

A Treasure Worth Keeping

by

Kathryn Springer

Available March
wherever books are sold.

Steeple Hill®

www.SteepleHill.com

LI87472

Love Inspired®

TITLES AVAILABLE NEXT MONTH

Don't miss these four stories in March

HEART'S HAVEN by Lois Richer
Pennies from Heaven
Cooking at the Haven, a new outreach mission in Chicago, was chef Cassidy Preston's way to pay back a huge favor. For Tyson St. John, the mission was a place to raise his nephew. Together they could make it their own haven as a family.

A TREASURE WORTH KEEPING by Kathryn Springer
Evie McBride planned a secluded summer running her dad's antique shop. But the teacher in her couldn't ignore a troubled teen who needed tutoring—or the teen's handsome uncle. Would this play-it-safe girl risk her heart for a treasure worth keeping?

MOUNTAIN SANCTUARY by Lenora Worth
Raising her son and running her B and B in rural Arkansas kept Stella Forsythe busy. She wasn't looking for romance until Adam Callahan came to town. The world-weary cop offered his services as a Good Samaritan. With a little prayer, he hoped they could find sanctuary in their budding love.

A SOLDIER'S FAMILY by Cheryl Wyatt
Wings of Refuge
Pararescue jumper Manny Pena had stuck his foot in his mouth when he'd met Celia Munoz. Now he was desperate to make amends. But Celia wasn't having it. Could his growing commitment to her and her troubled son begin to convince her that perhaps she should take her own leap of faith?

LICNM0208